Mercy Row
A Philadelphia Story

Harry Hallman

Octane Interactive, LLC
Publishing

www.mercyrow.com

ISBN: 0615814018
ISBN-13: 9780615814018

Dedication

Dedicated to my family. Nothing is more important. To my wife Duoc, son Bill, daughter Nancy, granddaughter Ava, Ava's mother Cindy, and my parents, Harry and Floss, siblings Bill and Roberta, and grandparents who lived their lives in North Philadelphia.

Special thanks go to Peter at FirstEditing for his outstanding editing assistance.

1

Hot streams of sweat rolled down Jacob's face, stinging his eyes. With every step he took, he thought his heart would burst. His muscles ached. His lungs burned. He knew he couldn't last much longer.

"Fuck them!" he thought, as he felt a searing pain in the back of his head. Then everything went black.

"Mom, I'm sleeping," Jacob moaned.

"Shut the fuck up you little prick."

"Mom," Jacob moaned again.

"The little shit thinks I'm his mother," the big man said, laughing.

"Come on Mom, leave me alone," Jacob pleaded again.

"I said Shut The Fuck Up. Or I'm going to stick your head in the shit pot and drown you." The big man gave Jacob a stinging backhand across his face.

The pain of the slap helped clear Jacob's head. At first he thought the man was the cop who was chasing him, but as his vision focused, all he could see was rotted teeth, a filthy beard, and an ugly face. He figured he was in Hell. The smell was unbearable.

Jacob struggled to get up but the big man's 320 pounds easily held him in place. Jacob, at five-foot-ten was big for a seventeen-year-old, but he was no match for this behemoth.

"He's got nothin', not even a fucking penny. You good for nothin' little cock sucker. Where's your money you little prick?" the big man barked as he slapped Jacob hard across the face again.

"Fuck you!" Jacob yelled as tears welled up in his eyes. He struggled to get free but couldn't move.

"Aw, look at this. The little shit's crying. Just like a little girl. Maybe you should be fucked, you little cunt." The big man pulled Jacob's pants down and rolled him over.

Fully awake now, Jacob realized he was in a jail cell. Fear immediately paralyzed him. He could do nothing under this powerful man's grip. "Leave me the fuck alone you cock sucker!" Jacob screamed.

"Shut up. You'll be the cock sucker soon," the big man said, laughing as he unbuttoned his fly.

Franklin Garrett was sitting on a wooden stool in the corner of the cell, quietly watching. He didn't want to get involved. Whenever he got involved in something that was not his business, it meant trouble.

But he couldn't let this one alone. Not this time.

"Hey pal, leave the kid alone."

There was no response. So Franklin repeated himself, this time louder.

"Hey pal, I said leave the kid the fuck alone!"

"Shut the fuck up and wait your turn. I'll be with you as soon as I take care of this little girl. I got plenty for both of you, pretty boy," the big man yelled.

Franklin was handsome—he was about six feet tall, muscular, and held a hint of a bad boy in his penetrating blue eyes. He had no problem attracting women of all types, but he preferred the ones who were married. They were less needy and more generous.

He slowly rose from the stool, picked it up, walked over to the big man, and calmly bashed the stool over his head. The stool made a loud splintering noise as it fell apart in his hands. The big man let out a startled groan and toppled to the cell floor, unconscious.

Franklin checked to see if the man was breathing. He placed a hand to the hulking man's mouth and felt a faint draft. Franklin simultaneously felt a sense of relief that the man was still alive, but he also felt a creeping foreboding, hoping he didn't wake up too soon.

Jacob scrambled to his feet, still scared, but in a rage. He stared hard at the man on the floor. "You Fucker!" he yelled as he kicked the big man in the groin. "Fucker, Fucker, Fucker!" He kicked the man three more times before Franklin pulled him away.

"Whoa! Take it easy, kid. If you kill him we'll never get out of this place," Franklin said.

Jacob twisted out of Franklin's grip and yelled, "Fuck you! Leave me alone."

"That's gratitude kid. Maybe you didn't notice, but you were about to become that man's wife. I can't imagine how that could have been pleasant," Franklin said.

"I didn't ask for your help," Jacob snapped back.

"Okay, take it easy. Calm down."

"I am calm," Jacob replied as he kicked the big man in the groin one more time.

"Christ," Franklin thought. "This kid's nuts."

"Hey what's going on in there?" A guard doing his rounds snapped.

"Don't know. This guy just let out a scream and fell to the floor," Franklin replied. "I think he had a heart attack or something."

"What's the blood on his head?" the guard asked.

"I guess he hit his head when he fell," Jacob said.

"What about that broken stool?" the guard asked.

"He was sitting on it and it broke when he fell," Franklin replied.

"Yeah, that must be it," the guard said sarcastically.

The guard blew a whistle and two more guards ran to the cell.

"Get him out of there and take him to the infirmary." The guard unlocked the door and the two men entered. They took hold of the big man's jacket collar and dragged him out of the cell and down the hall.

"Hey, you're Franklin Garrett, aren't you?" the guard asked.

"Yep, that would be me."

"Well, I'll be damned. I never expected to see someone like you in my jail," the guard said.

"Me neither," Franklin replied.

"I do some part-time guard work over at the construction site. What are you in for?" the guard asked.

"A little dispute with one of my contractors over plumbing."

Garrett had been an Army infantry Officer during the war and he had seen his share of action. The one thing he couldn't stand was insubordination. It had gotten people hurt, or worse. It was because of a sniveling coward that he was shot in the leg during the battle of Chateau-Thierry in 1918. When he returned to the U.S., he trained recruits for six months. After resigning his commission, he landed at Charles Byrne's building project, in his hometown of Philadelphia, as supervisor of construction.

The Captain of the Guard heard the commotion and came to see what was going on.

"What the fuck's going on, Peters?" the Captain asked.

"One of the prisoners passed out, Sir... Maybe a heart attack," the guard replied.

"Where is he?" the Captain asked.

"Infirmary," the guard replied.

"What cell is Franklin Garrett in?" the Captain asked.

"He's right here, Sir." The guard pointed at Garrett.

"And Jacob Byrne?" the Captain asked.

"The kid? Over there," the guard answered.

"Get them both out here!"

"Yes sir." The guard nodded and snatched Jacob up by the collar, marching him forward, toward the door. He looked at Garrett and cocked his head toward the cell door, saying, "You too. Let's go."

Jacob stumbled and fell as the guard dragged him to the door.

"Come on you little prick!" the guard yelled. "Ya want a beating?"

"Shut the fuck up you stupid ass," the Captain said. "That's Charles Byrne's son."

The guard suddenly let go of Jacob. "Shit kid, I didn't mean it. You alright?" The guard wasn't sure what to do, so he patted him on the head.

"Fuck you, cop!" Jacob replied pulling away.

"Your father's man is waiting for you outside. You and that Garrett can leave now," the Captain said.

"Good to have friends in high places," Garrett said as he headed for the door.

"And a father who has the cops in his pocket." Jacob looked at the Captain fiercely.

George Graham was standing by the open door to Byrne's Rolls Royce when Jacob and Garrett left the jailhouse. Graham was a tall and muscular man—one you would not like to meet in a dark alley. He had a scar starting at his right ear that ran to the center of his neck. His looks alone got him out of many fights, but more often than not, he enjoyed knocking people around. He was Byrne's driver and bodyguard and had been with Byrne since Byrne's days as a gunrunner in Cuba. He had proved his worth on a number of occasions.

"Hello, Jakey," Graham said.

"George, I asked you not to call me Jakey. It's Jacob. I'm not a kid anymore," Jacob said with irritation.

"Oh yeah. I forgot. Get the fuck in the car, Jakey. Your father's waiting," Graham said. "Garrett," Graham nodded to Franklin.

"Hello George," Franklin replied.

"You sit with me in the front," Graham ordered.

"Sure," Franklin answered. He knew better than to do anything other than what Graham asked. He had never met anyone who scared him as much as Graham.

"So you're Mr. Byrne's son. I didn't know he had kids," Franklin said to Jacob.

"Shut up," Graham ordered.

Byrne conducted most of his business out of his home—a large five-story mansion located on North Broad Street, just north of Fairmont Avenue.

It had been built sometime in the 1880s, but when Byrne had purchased it, he immediately modernized the Victorian home.

The Byrne mansion reeked of money. The home was at least four times wider than the row-homes Byrne had built for the blue-collar folks, and three stories taller. The brickwork was immaculate and the foyer was two stories high with a horseshoe stairway wrapping the elegant room gracefully. Byrne's office was on the first floor.

"Okay. Out," Graham barked. "Mr. Byrne's waiting for you in his office."

As Jacob and Garrett entered, Byrne growled. "Goddamn it, Jacob! What the hell were you thinking?"

Charles Byrne was a tall, slender man with graying dark brown hair, yet he had a commanding presence. He was born of a poor family in the inner city of Philadelphia. Byrne made his fortune before he was thirty, selling weapons to both the Spanish and the Cuban rebels during the Spanish-American War. In 1910, he returned to his hometown and invested his fortune into building row-homes in the growing northern part of the city. He had one son, Jacob, and no one else. Jacob's mother, Mercy Byrne, had died of the Spanish Flu in 1918 as so many others had. Like many rich men who had started in poverty, he had a certain distain for the poor class.

"I was thinking, Father, that asshole grease ball didn't need two watches," Jacob retorted.

"Are you nuts? You have a watch and I give you money every week. You don't need to steal," Byrne said in dismay.

"You don't get it, Pop. I like taking things from the grease balls. They come up here from South Philly and think they can sell their stolen crap. Well they can't," Jacob yelled.

Byrne backhanded Jacob.

"Go ahead, you old bastard. Hit me again," Jacob yelled.

Byrne hit him again.

"Stay away from the Italians! I don't need trouble with them. You little idiot, you know they control the brick layers," Byrne said as he hit Jacob again.

"Screw you!" Jacob yelled as he left the room, slamming the door on his way out.

Byrne shook his head in dismay and looked at Franklin.

"Garrett, get the fuck over here," Byrne bellowed.

Franklin, who had been sitting on an antique chair imported from France in the corner of the spacious office, slowly got up and walked over to Byrne's large desk. Byrne didn't ask him to sit.

"For Christ's sake, Garrett! You're the best manager I've had on this project, but I swear you are trying my patience. I can't afford to keep losing contractors. What happened this time?" Byrne asked.

"Mr. Byrne, I am here to see that these homes get built the way you want them built. The plumbing contractor was using just oakum and cement instead of lead to seal the waste pipe joints. If the inspectors see that, they'll make us redo everything. He gave me some lip so I showed him who was boss," Franklin explained.

"He was doing that because I told him to, you fucking hot head. Leave the inspectors to me," Byrne said. "Let me give you a little lesson in economics, Garrett. Maybe I'll be able to get something through that thick skull of yours. I have a contract to build 10 blocks of homes. Each block has 200 homes in it. That's 2000 homes. I sell these homes for $2,000 each. It costs me, on average, $1,400.00 to build each home. If I can cut on materials I can build them for less and make a better profit," Byrne explained.

"But what happens when these joints fail in a few years?" Franklin asked.

"What the fuck do you care? We'll be on the next project," Byrne said.

"But..."

"There are no buts. That's the way it is and if that troubles your sensibilities then get the fuck out and find another job," Byrne said irritably.

Franklin didn't answer.

After a pause, Byrne asked, "Well, what're you going to do, Garrett?"

"I am going to build your homes, Mr. Byrne," Franklin replied.

"Good. Get the fuck out of here and get back to work."

Leaving Byrne's office, Franklin raged inside. It wasn't the fact that they were doing a shoddy job building the homes. He could care less. It was that he just hated being treated like a low-life fool. Moreover, he hated the fact that he didn't do anything about it even more.

Jacob was sitting on the bottom step of the staircase as Franklin left Byrne's office. "Hey, Garrett?" Jacob called.

"What?"

"Thanks," Jacob said. "Sorry I was an asshole in the jail."

"You're right; you were an asshole," Franklin replied.

Jacob laughed and said, "Okay, okay. Let's kiss and make up." He stuck his hand out, offering it to Franklin. Franklin looked at Jacob's hand for a second and then grasped it and shook.

George Graham interrupted them as he threw a small bag to Jacob.

"Here, it's the money and watches you had on you when you were arrested," Graham said.

"Thanks, George. I thought they had gone to the Police Benevolent Association," Jacob said sarcastically.

Graham nodded to Garrett as he walked away.

"That guy scares me," Franklin said.

"He should," Jacob replied.

"Kid, I have a question for you. What's the deal with you and the Italians? Franklin asked.

"I'm not a kid. I'm seventeen, almost eighteen. And call me Jacob. It's not so much the grease balls I hate; it's their gang. They have South Philly under their control and I'll be damned if I let them have North Philly. That's my territory. Always has been," Jacob answered.

"Yours?" Franklin said, laughing. "What do you mean, 'yours'?"

"I'm sure you know my pop is building 2,000 homes just below Lehigh Avenue. What you might not know is that he already has contracts to build another 50,000 homes north of Lehigh over the next five years," Jacob said.

"Great. More work for me," Franklin said enthusiastically.

"Along with the houses he'll be building factories. Actually, the homes are being built to house the factory workers. So this area will be buzzing with workmen looking for a good time. Women, drinking and gambling. I'll give them what they want," Jacob explained.

"You do know that prostitution, booze and gambling are illegal," Franklin said.

"Exactly; that's why people pay more. It's a gold mine. And besides, it's a stupid law," Jacob said. "The grease balls are making a fortune in South Philly from booze and we got to keep them out of the North."

"Does your father know your plans?" Franklin asked.

"Fuck no. He's afraid the Italians will boycott laying bricks for his homes. You heard what he said," Jacob said.

"They will," Franklin said.

"So what! We'll hire the Irish," Jacob said.

"Well, it is a grand idea you have there, but without your father's money it won't be happening," Franklin stated.

"We'll see about that," Jacob replied. "There are other ways to get money."

"Like how?" Franklin asked.

"Like the grease balls," Jacob quipped.

Jacob looked at Franklin for a few seconds in silence, then said, "Mr. Garrett, my old man talks highly of you. And believe me, that means something. He doesn't think much of most people." He paused and said, "I have a proposition for you."

"Oh yeah?" Franklin asked.

"Yeah. If you take me under your wing and teach me the building business, when I take over for my father you'll be Number Two. I'll let you in on my other less... 'legal' enterprises," Jacob said.

"Take over for your father! And when do you think that will happen?" Franklin asked, laughing.

"Not sure, but it will happen someday," Jacob replied.

"You have some big brass balls kid," Franklin said.

"I know," Jacob replied.

"I'll think about it."

"Good. And since you'll be my partner I'll just call you Frank from now on," Jacob said.

"I said I'll think about it. Jesus H. Christ you're something else," Franklin said.

"I know," Jacob replied, smiling. "Oh, Frank! You want a watch? I have one already," Jacob tossed Franklin the watch he had taken from the Italian.

2

"Goddamn it, Frank! Stay down. Jesus Christ, you'd think you were never in the army. I don't know how the fuck you made it home alive," Jacob whispered.

"Funny boy. Watch your fucking mouth. You're not the boss yet," Franklin said.

"If you'd get your head out of your ass you might live to tomorrow, " Jacob replied.

"Stick it up your ass," Franklin said.

"That's the best you can do, Frank? Stick it up your ass! You're losing your touch, Boyo," Jacob said.

"Shut the fuck up. The truck is coming," Franklin said.

In the three years since Franklin had agreed to show Jacob the construction ropes, the two had developed an almost brotherly relationship. The good-natured yet gruff banter had become standard when they plied their other favorite profession of hijacking booze shipments that came from Kieran Leary's Atlantic City operation, en route to the local South Philly mobster Sal Sansone. It broke the tension.

Charles Byrne had not been happy about Jacob quitting school to come into the business, but he gave up when Jacob was kicked out of Northeast High in his senior year. Jacob had attended three private schools before Northeast, all of which had asked him to leave. Byrne was fed up, so he let Franklin take Jacob under his wing. It turned out that Jacob was a natural leader and a fast learner. In three years, Jacob's crews were the best at Byrne Construction.

Jacob had changed since he first met Franklin in jail three years earlier. He was taller and his rugged good looks reflected the man he had become. His body was hard and lean from building Byrne Construction's homes.

Byrne Construction had already built twenty thousand of the traditional three-bedroom, one-bath, two-story row homes along with several large factories. These new homes covered a huge area now, starting in the east at Kensington Avenue and stretching west to Fifth Street; in the south, the homes began at Leigh Avenue North and ended at Erie Avenue. Byrne had considerably increased his wealth through these efforts. He took every short cut he could to keep it.

Franklin raised his hand and pointed to the truck. In a moment, a large pine tree fell across the road.

"Okay, Jacob. You ready?" Franklin asked.

"Fuck yes," Jacob replied.

The truck stopped to avoid the tree.

"Okay… go!"

Franklin, Jacob and three of their crew jumped out of the dark, blasting their Thompson machine guns. As the .45 caliber bullets peppered the ground in front of the truck, the driver and his passenger pulled out their pistols.

"Don't be fucking idiots. Drop the heat. You don't want to die for a few bottles of booze, do you?" Jacob shouted.

The two men dropped their guns.

"Down," Franklin said, and the men complied.

"Fucking Micks. Do you know who we work for?" one of the men asked as he dropped to his knees.

"Yeah, we know. Some wop prick," Franklin said.

"You're dead. All of you. And your fucking Mick families," the man said.

"Shut the fuck up," Jacob said as he pressed the man's face to the ground with his boot. "You're scaring me." Jacob picked up the men's guns and put them in his waistband.

Franklin pointed to the truck and Jacob and his three men went to check the cargo. As Jacob opened the back flap, he was kicked in the face and went down hard. When he looked up, he was staring at a .38 revolver. A shot rang out.

The man fell onto Jacob and he quickly pushed him off.

"What the fuck. Am I shot?" Jacob yelled.

"No, I got him first," one of his men replied.

"Oh fuck. There's blood," Jacob said.

"No. That's his blood."

"Holy shit!" Jacob exclaimed as he felt his chest and stomach for wounds. "What's your name?"

"I'm Michael, Mike Kelly," he replied.

Mike Kelly was second generation American-Irish. His family lived in Kensington, where most of Jacob and Franklin's crew came from. It was a tough neighborhood and it created tough men and women. Kensington had been a magnet for the Irish immigrating to Philadelphia trying to find a better life. Most were hard-working people who were relegated as second-class citizens by the ruling protestants of English decent and they endured names meant to diminish them like "Natty," "Harp," or "Mick". Kensington also was the home of numerous Irish gangsters and tough guys. At the age of twenty, Mike Kelly was one of the toughest.

Just as Jacob had started learning the construction business, the Italian mob had tried to pressure Byrne Construction for protection money. No money, no Italian bricklayers. Charles Byrne was incensed and Jacob suggested he make a deal with the Irish bricklayers. Byrne talked to the Irish bricklayer's bosses, made a deal and told the Italians to stick their protection up their dago asses.

The Italians weren't very happy with this and started burning down homes in retaliation. So Byrne, at Franklin's suggestion, hired a crew of Irish hooligans to guard his construction sites. After a number of skirmishes and a couple of Italian deaths, the mob gave up on Byrnes. They had bigger fish to fry. Probation had opened a whole new world of opportunity.

Jacob convinced his father to keep the Irish security force, which included Mike Kelly, and these tough Irish thugs became the core of Franklin and Jacob's enforcement crew. Garrett and Jacob took the opportunity that prohibition offered them and began hijacking the Italian boss Sal Sansone's booze deliveries. They used the money to open a number of joints of their own, all of which were in North Philly between Lehigh Avenue in the south, and Allegheny Avenue in the north. They were also selling booze to a number of speakeasies and clubs throughout the North Philly area.

They didn't need to steal the Italian mob's booze any longer. They had made their own deals directly with Kieran and with the smugglers out of Dover Delaware. But Jacob enjoyed taking from the Italian mob. So they continued the hijacking.

"Mike, you're with me from now on. Get in the truck and drive," Jacob said. "And thanks."

Mike nodded and jumped in the driver's seat.

Jacob looked at Franklin, then down to the driver and his passenger who were still lying on the ground. Franklin slowly closed his eyes for a moment and held out his hands for Jacob to give him the Thompson. They had never killed their high-jacking victims before but these two men could identify them for killing their associate and it had to be done.

Jacob shook his head no and emptied his Thompson into the two men.

He got in the truck and said, "Mike, let's get the fuck out of here."

Franklin shook his head in amazement, grinned and said, "Drag them into the woods," Franklin ordered, pointing to the dead men. Once his men had done what he ordered he said. "Let's go, guys. Follow that truck."

This had been the first time anyone in Jacob's crew had killed someone. There had been a fair amount of roughing up their victims, but never a killing. Jacob's bravado belied how he felt inside. His gut was shaking and it was all he could do to not spew his guts all over the truck. Outwardly, he looked cool and collected.

Two days later Franklin and Jacob were in old man Byrne's office. "You fucking idiots! What the fuck were you thinking?" Byrne yelled.

"What are you talking about?" Jacob asked.

"You stupid little prick! Did you think I wouldn't find out what you and this dick face were up to?" Byrne replied, pointing to Franklin. "I can't believe you killed three of Sansone's men!"

Jacob looked at Franklin. "Killed! I have no idea what you're talking about," Jacob said incredulously.

"Oh come off it Jacob, I know what you two have been doing for a year now. And I don't care as long as it doesn't bring a shit storm on me," Byrne said.

"You don't have anything to worry about. First they don't know who we are and second if they did, we have a crew that can take care of them if they fuck with us," Jacob explained.

"If I know then they know, and you can be sure they won't take this lying down. It's one thing to rob them, but killing their men is something they cannot ignore," Byrne said.

"We didn't have a choice. One of them tried to kill Jacob. We killed him first. We couldn't leave the other two alive to finger us," Franklin said.

"Okay. Okay. Beef up your crew and be sure they all have weapons. And make sure the two of you take bodyguards wherever you go. If you need money I'll pay," Byrne said.

Jacob and Franklin looked at each other in surprise.

"Don't be so surprised. You're my son after all," Byrne said. After a pause he continued. "Oh, one other thing. You'll be working for me now through George Graham. I'll want my cut every month. You know, a man's gotta eat? Bring me a case of that Scotch you pilfered with my share from the heist."

3

A week after the Sansone gang member killings, Jacob delivered his father's share and a case of Mackinlay's Scotch Whiskey.

"How much did you have to give the old bastard?" Franklin asked Jacob.

"Three grand," Jacob replied.

"What the fuck? Are you kidding me? That's a third of our take!" Franklin bemoaned.

"I know! That old cheap prick is now our partner. Everything we make he gets a third. We have no choice. He has the connections and could have us shut down in minutes if he wanted," Jacob responded.

"But one-third for doing nothing? He gives a lecture and gets three grand in return and a partnership. That's just nuts!" Franklin said.

"Frank, he won't live forever and when he goes I get the construction business. And we get all of our business back. Meanwhile we need to step up our game to get him his fucking share," Jacob said.

"How long will that be? He's in his late forties. We'll have to wait ten years, maybe more," Franklin said.

"Maybe, but right now I need a drink. Let's go over to Mickey Mahoney's place on Girard Avenue," Jacob said.

"Mahoney, that fucking Pollack? Why his place? We can go to our place on Allegheny Avenue. There's a Jane there with a great chassis I'd like to play hide the sausage with," Franklin replied.

"You can hide your sausage anytime. I want to see how Mickey runs his joint. He sent a message that he might want to do some business with us. So I told him we would stop by tonight," Jacob said.

"Interesting," Franklin mused. "Why do you think Mahoney changed his name?"

"He's been playing around in Atlantic City where we Irish are in charge. He wants to fit in. You know, be a gangster. Like everybody doesn't know he's a Pollack!" Jacob replied, smiling.

"Yeah," Franklin said.

"Get Mike and Natty to come with us. My father is right. They might be looking for us," Jacob said.

"You think they know?" Franklin asked.

"Not sure, but better to be safe than sorry."

"Okay; good idea. I'll be back in twenty minutes," Franklin said.

The drive to Mickey Mahoney's speakeasy was only fifteen minutes. Mahoney's place was on the second floor of a row of houses on West Girard Avenue near Front Street. These style homes had the nickname of "Father, Son and Holy Ghost" because they were three stories instead of the two-story homes Byrne was building north of Lehigh Avenue. Mahoney had bought up the entire block and kept the appearance of a residential community. He took out the walls on the second floor of all the homes to create a large speakeasy.

To get to the second floor you had to go through the house in the middle of the block and walk up the stairs. Then, it was all gambling, booze and women. The third floor had the rooms for his prostitution business and the first floor was for storage. These homes also had basements where he brewed beer. It was a sweet operation and one that was protected by bribes and the fact that most local police didn't consider gambling, booze and prostitution a real crime.

Mike had Natty, the driver, park the car down the street from Mahoney's joint. Natty and Mike got out of the car first to check if all was secure. Once he was satisfied that it was safe, he motioned for Jacob and Franklin to exit. They got out of the car, looked around and started walking to the entrance to Mahoney's speakeasy. When they were halfway there, a car came up behind them and as it neared, Mike pushed Jacob and Garrett to a crouching position behind a parked car.

"Get down!" Mike yelled.

As the car passed by the woman passenger and her kid looked at them.

"Mike? What the fuck!" Franklin bellowed.

"Sorry boss! I thought…" Mike replied as Jacob interrupted him.

"It's okay, Mike. Frank—he's doing his job," Jacob explained.

"I know, but for Christ's sake he scared the shit out of me," Franklin said.

"Better that than a bullet between your eyes," Jacob said.

" Okay, Okay. You're right."

They continued to the speakeasy door and knocked. The doorman peeked out of a small window and unlocked the door. Franklin, Jacob, Mike and Natty started up the narrow steps. As they reached the top, there was a cacophony of sounds of men talking, women giggling, and bottles rattling all to the tune of ragtime being played by the house piano player. The smell was a mixture of stale beer, whiskey, sweat, tobacco and perfume.

The left side of the large room was where the gaming tables were located. There were a couple of Poker tables, a Roulette wheel, Blackjack and Craps tables. The right side was for the bar and the women. Most of the women were for hire, but on occasion, some of the local Philly straight gals would stop by to see where the action was. You could tell them from the girls-for-hire because the straight gals had their clothes on.

Mickey Mahoney was sitting at the bar close to the stairs.

"Mickey! Jacob said. "How's it hanging?"

"Jacob!" Mickey replied as he took Jacob's hand.

"Hello Frank," Mickey said as he shook Franklin's hand. "Who're the harps?"

"This is Mike and Natty. They're friends of ours," Jacob said.

"What the fuck does that mean; harps? You a fucking Left-legger?" Mike said as he gave Mahoney the eye.

"Take it easy, Mike. Mickey's a Pollack," Jacob said.

"What the fuck? A Pollack with an Irish name?" Mike asked as he spat on the floor.

"Who gives a shit? We're here to have fun, right? Mike?" Franklin asked in a commanding manner.

"Yeah," Mike said as he loosened his tightened fists.

"Mike, take Natty over and introduce him to some pussy, will you?" Jacob said.

"Yeah," Mike replied. "Come on Natty."

"You come into my place and insult me," Mickey said as he stared at the two men walking away.

"No trouble, no insult, Mickey. Just here to discuss business," Franklin said.

"Well keep your fucking dogs on a leash," Mickey said.

"Shut the fuck up, Mickey. You invited us here. What the fuck did you want to talk about?" Jacob asked.

"We'll talk business later when you cool down. Come back next week," Mickey said.

"Fuck you. You want to talk, you come to us next time," Jacob growled.

"Give these two 'Skurwiel' a beer on me," Mickey said as he walked away.

"Skurwiel, what's that mean, you prick?" Jacob yelled. "What's that mean, Frank?"

"How the hell am I supposed to know? I guess it means 'swell guys' in Pollack," Franklin said, laughing. "I'm here to get some giblets and I see some good ones over there."

Franklin nodded over to a group of scantily clad prostitutes. The bar tender put two beers on the table.

"I don't like it, that fucking Pollack," Jacob said.

"Take it easy. Come get a whore with me," Franklin said.

"Nah, I'll just drink my beer. You go ahead."

"Your loss. Getting that thing between your legs straightened out might do your disposition good," Franklin said as he grabbed his beer and strode off.

"Hey buddy, give me a shot of the good whiskey will you?" Jacob asked the bartender.

"Sure, here," the bartender said as he placed the shot glass on the bar and poured the whiskey.

"Nice tat," Jacob said to the bartender. "What is it?"

"Souvenir from the Navy when I was in Hong Kong. It means 'Good Luck' in Chinaman talk," the bartender said.

Jacob picked up the shot, dropped it in the beer, and drank the beer in one long swallow.

"Another," Jacob said.

Jacob knew that Mickey Mahoney had been doing good business at this location, but he had not realized how good. Mahoney had to be making at least a grand a night. Over three hundred large a year was a very good payday. He had been looking to get established below Lehigh Avenue and this would be the perfect place.

Jacob finished his boilermaker and walked over to where Franklin, Mike and Natty were being fawned over by the three whores and a couple of straight gals.

"Guys, let's scram," Jacob ordered.

"What the fuck? We were just getting started," Franklin protested as he stood up.

"This place gives me the willies. Let's go over to our place at K and A. You can take care of that bulge in your pants there," Jacob said.

"Shit! Better hurry; I don't know how much longer I can keep it up," Franklin said, smiling. "Natty, get the car, will you?"

"Right-o, Frank," Natty replied and headed out.

Jacob, Franklin and Mike started for the door, and discussed the virtues of Mickey's whores compared with their own whores.

"Mickey's got a pretty good operation going here. The gals are Hotsy-Totsy and the place is full," Franklin said.

"What the fuck is hotsy-totsy?" Jacob asked.

"You know, good looking, pleasing to the eye. All the college kids say it," Franklin answered.

"College kids? You're a grown man, Frank. How the hell do you learn college kid talk?" Jacob asked.

"I date the Dean of Temple's wife. She keeps me up on things. And she keeps me up," Frank said as he laughed.

"You mean you fuck her. You never date, like, normal people," Jacob said.

Jacob and Franklin continued their banter as Mike led the way down the stairs to the doorway outside.

"It's fucking cold out here. Where's Natty?" Franklin asked.

"He's coming, Frank. He had to walk up the street to get the car," Mike replied.

As he was talking, Mike noticed a car coming east on Girard and grabbed Jacob's arm.

"It's okay Mike. Look. It's just that kid and his family we saw when we came in," Jacob said.

Mike saw it first. As the car was coming up on them a barrel of a shotgun appeared in the open window. Mike immediately pushed Jacob to the ground as he yelled "Gun!" and pulled his .38 from his coat pocket.

Franklin reacted quickly and hit the ground behind a parked car. Several shotgun blasts riveted the car and ground around Jacob. Jacob crawled quickly behind the parked car with Franklin, as Mike returned fire.

Two men exited the car while pumping several more blasts from their shotguns in Mike's direction. Mike fired again and hit one of the men in the forehead. The back of the man's head exploded, spilling brains and blood back into the car. A woman screamed. The second man came around the front of the car yelling, "Sal says hello!" as he shot again, and missed.

Natty had seen what had happened as he was bringing the car around and put his foot down hard on the accelerator, headed straight for the gunman and the car he had gotten out of. The man turned, but it was too late. The impact of Natty's car with the gunman's squeezed the gunman between them, crushing his legs. The man screamed in a frenzy and pointing his shotgun at Natty, squeezed the trigger. At the same time, Mike ran up to the man and pumped two bullets in the side of his head.

Franklin ran to the car with his gun ready. In the back seat, there was a woman and a young boy.

"Who the hell are you?" he yelled at the woman.

The woman was screaming and incoherent. "They... they... oh my god, they..."

"Okay calm down," Franklin said.

Jacob joined Franklin at the car and looked at the boy. He said, "Kid, are you okay?"

"Yes sir, I'm okay," the kid replied.

"What's your name?" Jacob asked.

"Jimmy," the kid replied.

"Jimmy, I'm Jacob and everything's going to be fine." After a moment, Jacob asked, "How old are you, Jimmy?"

"Almost ten. Can you help my Mom?" Jimmy asked.

"Sure. Frank, get the woman. Mike, how's Natty?" Jacob asked.

"Dead. Took it in the face," Mike replied.

"Shit..." Jacob's voice lowered. "See if you can find a car so we can get out of here."

Mike ran down the street to find a car. Franklin, the woman, Jimmy and Jacob followed.

"Jacob, the cops will know it's your car," Franklin said.

"We'll be okay. I have friends in this precinct. My father's friends," Jacob replied.

Mike motioned them into a car he had hotwired.

The woman had calmed down some but was still sobbing and couldn't talk.

"Hey kid, how come you were in that car?" Franklin asked.

"This is Frank and that's Mike driving. We're friends. Nobody's going to hurt you," Jacob said.

"My Grandma kicked us out of the house yesterday and we didn't know where to go. We had to sleep in a park down near the high school last night. My mom said there was a place on Market Street that took care of homeless people so we were walking there," Jimmy said.

"Where's your father?" Jacob asked.

"My mom said he went to the war, but he didn't come back," Jimmy replied.

"I'm sorry about your dad, Jimmy. Go on," Jacob said.

"We were on Front Street and those two men said they would give us a ride to the homeless place. My mom didn't want to go with them, but they made us. They didn't take us to the place. They just rode up and down the street," Jimmy said.

"Okay, Jimmy. Thanks. You try to rest now. You and your mom will stay with me tonight. I'm going to talk to Frank now," Jacob said. "Mike, pull up at that gas station at Front and Lehigh."

The gas station was closed when Mike pulled in. Franklin and Jacob got out.

"Mike, stay here with them, will you?" Jacob asked.

"Sure," Mike replied as he got out of the car and stood by the driver's side door with his pistol in his hand.

Jacob guided Franklin away from the car as he said, "How the fuck did they know we were here? Did you mention to anyone we were going to Mickey's?"

"No. I don't think so. I picked up Mike and Natty and came to get you," Franklin said.

"Mahoney. That fucking bastard. How else would they have known we were going to Mahoney's place?" Jacob asked, his anger rising.

"Why, though? What's in it for him if we get hit?" Franklin asked.

"Pay off, control of North Philly. I don't know," Jacob said. "We'll talk this over later. Let's get the woman and kid to the house."

Jacob and Franklin started walking back to the car. "How about that kid?" Franklin asked. "Cool as a cucumber. I would have been shitting my pants at his age."

"Yeah," Jacob replied, and then said to Mike, "Take us home."

"You got it boss," Mike replied.

Jacob's house wasn't far from where they were. Frank and Jacob had refitted eight of the seventeen houses on the row of homes at Howard and Wishart Streets. Mike took four and Frank had four. They broke through walls creating larger rooms for sleeping and entertaining. Each was now about 4,000 square feet of living space, as opposed to the single homes being just 1,000 square feet.

The only area they couldn't open up were the basements, which were originally dirt walls and floors and provided the foundation of the homes. Instead they had the walls plastered and concreted the floors. They were now individual storage areas. This is where they stored their booze before delivering it to their customers throughout North Philly. The small 8x16 foot yards had access from an alleyway between the row homes on Wishart Street and those on Allegheny Avenue. This gave them easy and somewhat private access to the basements from the yard.

Not that privacy mattered all that much. All the homes on the row were housed by members of Jacob and Franklin's crew as were the row homes on the south side of Wishart Street. This made for a one-block fortress that protected their stock and their person.

They originally had a double-open doorway between each other's homes, but Jacob had doors and locks installed because he got tired of Garrett's legions of so-called girlfriends wandering into his area. Garrett was the horniest man Jacob had ever met. Not that Jacob didn't like women; it was just that he valued his privacy more.

Mike pulled up to 125 Wishart Street where the shared entrance to Garrett's and Jacob's home was located. There was parking on both sides of the small street, making it difficult to park. That was never a problem for Franklin and Jacob as their neighbors knew that the spots in front of their homes were to be left open.

"Okay Jimmy, we're home. Mrs. ... I am sorry, what's your name?" Jacob asked.

"Molly. Molly Simms," she replied.

"Mrs. Simms, we're home. You can stay here until you can make other arrangements. You and Jimmy are safe with us. Come on, let's go in," Jacob said.

"Mike, make sure we have men at each corner and in the alley. We'll see you in the morning. Let's block the entrances with cars," Franklin said.

"Okay boss," Mike replied.

Mrs. Reilly, who had shared responsibility as housekeeper for both Jacob and Franklin, met them at the door. Mrs. Reilly was in her late forties and a bit stout with a very pleasant face. Like many of the Kensington Irish women, you could never take a pleasant face for a lack of strength. Mrs. Reilly reared seven children after her husband was killed in a bar fight when her youngest child Sean was only two years old. One of her boys was a police officer, another was a priest, and one was in prison for armed robbery. The youngest worked for Jacob. Her three daughters were all married and lived near Kensington Avenue and Front Street.

"My, my, Mr. Byrne; what have we here?" Mrs. Reilly asked.

"Mrs. Reilly, please call me Jacob. My father is Mr. Byrne," Jacob said.

"Alright Mr... ah... Jacob," Mrs. Reilly replied.

Jacob knew that the next day Mrs. Reilly would be back to calling him Mr. Byrne. She was a stubborn woman. He had once tried to get her to use a new electric vacuum cleaner, but she refused to use it. She said it didn't get the carpet as clean as a good beating did. The electric cleaner was sitting in the kitchen closet gathering dust.

"This is Molly and Jimmy Simms. They are in need of assistance for a few days. Mrs. Simms, Jimmy, meet Mrs. Reilly," Jacob said.

"And may God help you," Franklin remarked laughingly to Molly.

"And what do you mean by that, Mr. Garrett?" Mrs. Reilly asked in mock anger. "God should be helping you. Out every night till the wee hours drinking and God knows what."

She looked at the mother and son, and said, "Molly, bring Jimmy along and we'll get you both a hot bath and a warm bed. Do you have a change of clothes?" she asked.

"We did, Miss. But we lost them," Jimmy said.

"No matter, we'll go shopping tomorrow and get your mom and you something suitable," Mrs. Reilly said as she glanced at Jacob and rubbed her thumb and forefinger together.

"Have you had anything to eat?" Mrs. Reilly asked.

"Not since dinner. I could use a sandwich," Franklin said.

Not you, you big lug. I was talking to Molly and Jimmy," Mrs. Reilly chastised.

"Well, excuse me. I just own the place," Franklin said.

"And I run it," Mrs. Reilly said with an "and you know it" smile on her face. "Come along all of you. I'll whip something up. We'll get you that bath after you eat."

In the normal row home, the kitchen was a small affair that included a stove, a sink, an icebox and a table. In Jacob and Franklin's modified homes the kitchen was twice that size and had a Kelvinator refrigerator that cost over $700, and the latest Magic Chef gas stove. In the dining room there was a table that could accommodate twelve people.

"How about some Taylor's Ham sandwiches? I picked up some fresh Kaiser rolls from the German bakery this afternoon," Mrs. Reilly said.

"My favorite," Franklin said.

"Okay, have a seat and I'll whip some up. Use the dining room. I don't like anybody in my kitchen when I am cooking," Mrs. Reilly said.

"Yes sir, sergeant Reilly!" Franklin said, as he saluted and went to the dining room.

"Coffee?" Mrs. Reilly asked.

"That would be great," Jacob said.

"Go wash your hands," Mrs. Reilly ordered.

After washing their hands Molly, Jimmy, Garrett and Jacob sat down at the table. The savory flavor of the Taylor's Ham mixed with the aroma of brewing coffee filled the room and fueled their hunger. The wife of a local ward leader introduced Franklin Garrett, when he first moved back to Philadelphia, to Taylor's Ham. She told him it was made from pork and was the best breakfast food. He told her she was the best breakfast food and proved it several times that morning. He never saw her again, but every time he ate Taylor's Ham, it reminded him of that night.

"Okay, here we go," Mrs. Reilly said as she placed a large platter of Kaiser Roll and Taylor Ham sandwiches on the table. She left and retuned with cups, coffee and dark German mustard.

"Go on, Jimmy. Grab yourself a sandwich before Mr. Garrett eats them all. You too Molly," Mrs. Reilly said.

For the first time that evening, Jacob studied Molly. She was maybe twenty-five years old and must have been married young to have a nine-year-old son. Molly had light blonde hair and dark brown eyes. She had a slender body and small breasts.

"Molly, may I call you Molly? Jacob asked.

"Yes sir, you may," Molly replied.

"Molly, Jimmy tells me your husband was in the war," Jacob said.

"Yes… he was killed in France. Excuse me," Molly replied as she wiped the tears from her eyes.

"I'm sorry, Molly. I didn't mean to bring up bad memories," Jacob said.

"No, no… you have been so nice to us. You deserve to know who we are," Molly said.

"Okay Molly, if it is not too hard on you," Jacob said.

"I was fifteen and my husband James was twenty-one when we were married. Both of us were from **Gloucester County** in Jersey. We moved to Philadelphia so James could work at the Artloom Mill on Lehigh Avenue," Molly explained.

"I know that building," Jacob said.

"Well, in 1917, James had to register for the draft and was selected shortly after. He was sent to France in 1918 and was killed near the Marne River. Jimmy and I had no money and no place to go so we asked James's mother if we could stay with her until we got on our feet. I got a job at a laundry, but I could never make enough to get my own place," Molly said.

"Jimmy said she kicked you out. Why'd she do that?" Jacob asked.

"Mrs. Simms is a hard woman. She took to beating Jimmy with a barber's strap when she thought he needed discipline. I begged her not to and finally we got into a big fight yesterday. She kicked us out…" Molly's eyes welled red with tears. "What kind of women does that?" Molly asked, crying.

"It's okay, Molly. You have a place now and you and Jimmy can stay as long as you need to. No reason for tears," Jacob said.

"Thank you, Mr. Byrne. I just don't know what to say," Molly said.

"The first thing is we will never speak of what happened tonight to anyone. Got it, Jimmy?" Jacob asked.

"Yes sir," Jimmy said

"Never," Molly said.

"Second thing. Call me Jacob. Now eat up. I see Frank is on his third sandwich. If you wait any longer there won't be any left," Jacob said.

4

Mike brought the car around the next morning, parked in front of 125 West Wishart and walked to the corner of Front and Wishart where two of the crew were stationed.

"Hiya, boys. How's it going?" Mike asked.

"All quiet," one of the men said.

"I want you to bring the Packard around to block the street. That Ford is too small. I'll send Davie and Jack to relieve you," Mike said.

"Right-o, Mike."

Mike walked to the Howard and Wishart Street corner to see if the guards were awake. After that, he walked back to Jacob's house and knocked. Mrs. Reilly peeked out the window and let him in.

"Good morning, Mike," Mrs. Reilly said.

"Morning Mrs. Reilly. How are you?"

"Tip top, Mike," Mrs. Reilly replied.

"By the way, Sean's over on Lippincott, working on some repairs. When he's done I told him to stop by and see you," Mike said.

"Thank you, Mike. I never see that boy anymore. He's too busy to check in on his old mom," Mrs. Reilly said. "Mike, will you join us for breakfast?"

"For your breakfast, any day. Thank you," Mike replied.

Mike and Mrs. Reilly walked into the kitchen where Mike grabbed a cup of coffee and went to the dining room. No one had arrived yet, so he sat down and asked, "What are we having today, Mrs. Reilly?"

"Scrapple, eggs and toast. I've got some nice Danish. Some butter cake and a slab of crumb cake as well," Mrs. Reilly replied.

"Where's everyone?" Mike asked.

"They'll be down soon enough," Mrs. Reilly replied.

Franklin was the first to arrive and took his normal spot at the end on the table. It was a kind of ritual with him. He took one side of the table, the one closer to his home and Jacob the other side. He joked with Jacob that he was in the wife's chair since he, Franklin, was far too maschio to sit in the wife's chair.

"Morning, Mike. You check on the guards?" Franklin asked.

"Yeah. All's good," Mike replied.

"Good. What's the old crone cooking up this morning?" Franklin asked loudly so Mrs. Reilly could hear.

"I heard that," Mrs. Reilly said.

"I know. You hear everything. What's cooking?" Franklin asked.

"Scrapple," Mike answered.

"What the hell is scrapple, anyway?" Franklin asked.

"It's pork, Frank. The bits and pieces they don't use for the good meat. They mix it up with spices and cornmeal. It's Dutch or something," Mike said.

"What do you mean bits and pieces?" Franklin asked.

"You don't want to know," Mike replied.

"Well whatever it is made of, it's damn good. Mrs. Reilly, be sure mine is thin and crispy," Franklin said.

First Jacob arrived, then Molly and Jimmy. The meal was a feast for Molly and Jimmy and they ate as if they hadn't eaten in weeks. This pleased Mrs. Reilly. When they were finished eating Molly and Mrs. Reilly washed the dishes and put them away. Molly returned and sat in the chair closest to Jacob.

"Mr. Byrne, may I see you in the kitchen?" Mrs. Reilly asked.

"Frank, I don't know why I try to change that woman. It can't be done," Jacob said. "Sure Mrs. Reilly. Coming,"

"We're going to need some money to go shopping. Molly needs a couple of dresses and Jimmy needs some pants and shirts," Mrs. Reilly said.

Jacob pulled out a wad of cash, peeled off a $5 bill and handed it to Mrs. Reilly. She held her hand and kept it there, waiting. Jacob pulled a $20 bill and placed in her hand. Still she didn't move.

"Frank, Mrs. Reilly wants to see you in the kitchen," Jacob said.

Once Mrs. Reilly had extracted the proper amount of money from Jacob and Franklin, she gathered up Molly and Jimmy and started on their shopping spree, followed by two of Jacob's men. They didn't have to walk far. Front Street above Allegheny Avenue was a treasure chest of variety of stores. There was old Mr. Gold's shoe store, Seinfeld's five and dime cent store, Mrs. Johnson's ladies store and Pinky's children's store. There was also a butcher, a bakery, a fish store, a drug store, and furniture store on the street. If you couldn't find what you wanted on Front Street you could walk a mile or so to the east to Kensington and Allegheny Avenues where there were stores of every conceivable type.

As the group approached Front Street, Mrs. Reilly pointed out the American Store, on the right, where you could buy all manner of food. "We'll stop there on the way back and I'll pick up fixings for lunch. Jimmy, do you like TastyKakes?" Mrs. Reilly asked.

"Oh yes. Juniors are the best," Jimmy replied.

"Okay, we'll get you some TastyKake Juniors and then I am going to treat you to something I make for my children," Mrs. Reilly said.

"Oh! Oh! What is it?" Jimmy asked excitedly.

Mrs. Reilly had hoped Jimmy would ask. She was proud of her con- coction. "First we start with some German Rye Bread. The good kind from the German bakery on Clearfield Street. Then when we go to the American store I'll buy some American cheese, some Lebanon Baloney, some Jewish pickles, and my special ingredient, some Wise Potato Chips."

"What's a Potato Chip?" Jimmy asked.

"Oh! You've never had a potato chip?" Mrs. Reilly asked.

"No," Jimmy replied.

"Well you are in for a treat. Some smart fella' thought up the idea of slic- ing a potato into very thin slices and frying them until they are very crispy. He then put salt on them," Mrs. Reilly said. "When we get home I'll cut up the rye bread and spread some dark mustard on it. Then I'll put the Lebanon Baloney and cheese on the bread. I'll add a few slices of Kosher Pickle. After that, I'll take a big bunch of Potato Chips and lay it on top. I'll put another piece of rye bread on top and squeeze it down. How's that sound, Jimmy?"

"I'm hungry," Jimmy said.

"Jimmy, you just ate," Molly said.

"Oh, he's a growing boy, Molly. Mine used to eat me out of house and home. Especially my youngest, Sean," Mrs. Reilly said as they rounded the corner to Front Street and crossed Allegheny Avenue.

Sean Reilly was twenty-one, tall and solidly built. His blond hair was cut short and parted down the middle. He had been a problem student and Mrs. Reilly asked Jacob if he could put him to work in the construction busi- ness. Sean became a plumber and a good one. He often had to do repairs that no one else could. Today he was working on a home on Lippincott Street that had a stoppage.

When he finished he walked around to Wishart Street to see his mother. Four of Jacob's men were standing behind a 1920 Desoto sedan that blocked the entrance to the street. Sean knew them and stopped for some small talk. At about the same time an ice truck turned onto Wishart Street from Mascher Street just one block west of where Sean was talking to his friends. Nobody paid much attention, as it was common for ice trucks to make deliveries to the homes that had to fill their iceboxes daily.

The truck came half way down the street and started to accelerate. Before the men could react, the truck hit the Desoto and drove it forty feet down the street. It crushed one of Jacob's men and drove Sean Reilly head-first into the curb. He died instantly. Jacob's three remaining men opened fire and killed the driver and his passenger.

Jacob and Franklin had been sitting in Jacob's office, discussing plans for retaliation against Sal Sansone when they heard the shooting.

"Grab the guns, Jacob. Out the back door and into the alley. We'll flank them," Franklin said.

Jacob and Franklin ran to the back door and into the yard. As they did, machine gun fire sprayed bullets into the fence and the yard in front of them. They both dove for the ground behind the fence. This was not a safe spot.

"Frank! We need to get back into the house. I'll cover you. When I start shooting, run for the door," Jacob said.

"Do you know where they are shooting from?" Franklin asked.

"Yeah—second-floor window. The house directly across the alley. Okay… ready? Go!" Jacob said.

Jacob stood up, a .45 in each hand, and started shooting. Franklin ran and reached the door just as the machine gun started blasting again. A bullet grazed the calf of his leg as he rolled into the doorway and behind the wall. Jacob ducked back down.

"Frank! You alright?" Jacob yelled.

"Motherfucking son-of-a-bitch! I got it in the same fucking leg," Franklin said. I'm okay… just a graze."

"Well… I'm waiting! I could use some help here," Jacob yelled.

"Hold on. I'm getting a Thompson," Franklin said as he crawled into the dining room and opened the secret door in the closet, where he had a stash of several Thompson machine guns. He grabbed one, crawled back and said, "You ready?"

The shooter sprayed another round of fire.

"For fucking Christ's sake, yes! Shoot, will you!" Jacob replied.

Garrett broke the kitchen window and let loose the Thompson on the second-story window. Jacob ran to the door and rolled into the house unharmed.

"You okay?" Franklin asked.

"Yeah," Jacob replied. "Grab the broom and hold it up to the windows. Let's see if we can get them to shoot at it. I'll get by the door and when they shoot I'll blast them. Slide the Thompson over."

Franklin slid the Thompson to Jacob and got ready to lift the broom to the window. They heard shots. *Bang! Bang! Bang!* Pistol shots. The second-story window shattered with the impact of the shooter crashing through. He fell on the back porch roof and rolled off into the yard.

"It's okay, boss. We got him," a voice yelled out.

"Who's we?" Franklin yelled.

"It's me. Mike."

Franklin looked at Jacob, pursed his lips and blew out in a sigh of relief.

Mike had been checking on the guards in the alley at the Front Street entrance when he heard the shooting. He saw where it was coming from, ran around to Allegheny Avenue and broke in the front door of the house. There was a woman lying dead on the living room floor, her throat cut. It wasn't hard to determine which room the shooter was in. The Thompson made a lot of noise. He kicked down the door and shot three times and blew the man out the window.

"Frank, stay here and look after your wound. I'm going to see who the shooter was," Jacob said. Then he entered the yard, opened the yard door and climbed over the neighbor's fence.

The shooter was lying in a twisted heap in the middle of the yard. Half of his face was missing, but there was no mistaking the tattoo on the man's hand.

Jacob returned to the house. "How's the leg?" he asked.

"It's nothing; just a scratch. Luck of the Irish, I guess. How's the shooter?" Franklin asked.

"Let's just say he won't have an open casket," Jacob replied.

"Fuckin' Ginnies! That cunt Sansone needs a lesson," Franklin said.

"It was Sansone who ordered it, I am sure, but it was Mahoney's men who hit us," Jacob said.

"How the fuck do you know that?" Franklin asked.

"The shooter was the bartender from Mahoney's joint," Jacob answered.

"That motherfucking, cock sucking, Pollack!" Franklin shouted.

"We'll deal with both of them later, but first we need to explain this to the police," Jacob said.

Mike left the house the shooter was using and circled around to where the truck had slammed into the Desoto. People from the other block of Wishart were out **GAWKING** at the mess. Jacob's guys were out of their houses with their guns at the ready. Five men had taken up posts, protecting the entrance to Jacob's and Franklin's homes. The others were at the two entrances to the street.

"Two dead, Mike. Tim O'Hare and Sean Reilly," one crew member said.

"Fuck! Leave everything as it is. The cops will be here soon. You don't know nothing. Let Jacob and Frank do the talking," Mike said as he left to report to Jacob.

As Mike walked the short distance to the home's entrance, he wondered how they would tell Mrs. Reilly the news. This was going to be hard—very hard. Mike loved that old lady. His own mother had died when he was ten years old and he saw in Mrs. Reilly the mother he missed.

5

The Reilly funeral was a large affair. The killing of Sean Reilly, Tim O'Hare, and Natty Donahue incensed the Irish community of Kensington and a large number attended their wakes to pay their respects. Like many Irish wakes, there was plenty of food and drink and the longer the wake continued the angrier the crowd became. They blamed the Italians in South Philly and they wanted revenge. What they didn't know was that it was Mickey Mahoney's men, many of whom were also Irish. They had implemented the attack that the Italian mob had instigated. Not that it mattered. They wanted their revenge paid in blood and it would be the South Philly Italians who would pay the tab. Any South Philly Italians.

The last straw was when Mrs. Reilly threw herself on Sean's coffin, weeping. Witnessing her grief fueled the revenge lust on the part of the community and it boiled over, resulting in ten carloads of Irish men driving to South Philly on a hunt. They attacked seven Italian men, killing one of them. Not one of these men were with the Italian mob.

The next evening the Italians retaliated, injured twelve Kensington Irish men, and killed two. The police stepped up patrols on the main streets connecting North and South Philadelphia, Front Street and Delaware Avenue, stopping all suspicious vehicles. This did not stop the tension or the attacks. It got so bad that after a week, **Bishop Dougherty**, the Arch Bishop of the Philadelphia Archdiocese, threatened excommunication for anyone perpetrating these attacks. Both the Italians and most of the Kensington Irish were Roman Catholics and the threat, as hollow as it was, worked to abate the tension. In all, five men were killed and thirty hospitalized.

None of the attacks were perpetrated by Jacob's or Sal Sansone's gangs, both of whom were on lockdown. Mickey Mahoney was also in hiding. Jacob and Franklin were biding their time and planning a reprisal.

"What the fuck, Jacob? It's been three weeks and we're just sitting around jerking off. We need to hit them now!" Franklin said.

"I agree with Frank," Mike added. "We're looking like a bunch of punks. For Christ's sake they killed Tim and Sean!"

"Calm the fuck down. We're going to get them, I promise. We just have to give it some time and make them think we're chickens. Once they let their guard down... Bang!" Jacob said, holding his hand in the shape of a pistol.

"Yeah; and when's that?" Franklin asked.

"Next week. My connections tell me that Sansone is badmouthing us. Calling us weak. It's a good sign. He doesn't think we will hit back," Jacob said. "And that fuck Mahoney is in AC, hiding out with his Number Two, McCurdy. We'll take a little ride down there to get some fresh air. When we leave, Mahoney won't be a problem anymore."

"How do you know that?" Mike asked.

"We have somebody in on the inside," Franklin replied.

"Oh. Smart buggers, aren't you?" Mike asked in amazement.

The trio discussed their plans for an hour or so when Mrs. Reilly interrupted them. Mrs. Reilly had, of course, taken Sean's murder very badly. Jacob had his doctor sedate her the day they told her the horrific news and she had been under the doctor's care for a week. After Sean's funeral, Jacob insisted she take some time off. She was reluctant, but Jacob insisted and paid her full wages during the time she was absent from her work. Molly took up the slack, cleaning and making the meals. She was a good homemaker and made both Franklin and Jacob feel at ease.

"Jacob, Franklin, may I speak with you?" Mrs. Reilly asked as she entered the room with Molly.

Jacob, Franklin and Mike got to their feet and took turns kissing Mrs. Reilly's cheek. She looked thinner and older than she had before Sean's death. The strain was taking its toll. Her black dress was as wrinkled as her brow. This was not the Mrs. Reilly Jacob knew and loved; the pillar of strength, the fastidious woman who brought order to his life.

"Mrs. Reilly, how are you doing?" Jacob asked.

"I'm not doing well, Jacob. I sit around all day and think and think and it is driving me crazy. I must come back to work or I surely will be placed in Byberry," Mrs. Reilly said.

"First of all, I would never allow you to be put in that rat hole of a place. And secondly you're much too strong a woman for that to happen," Jacob replied.

"Well, thank you Jacob, but Sean was my youngest and it is just driving me mad," Mrs. Reilly said as she broke down in tears.

Molly took Mrs. Reilly's hand, softly patting it. Jacob pulled Mrs. Reilly close and buried her face in his chest. He could not imagine the pain that could do to such a powerful woman. He had felt pain when his mother died—a lot of pain. But he gradually began to move on. He thought of her frequently and when he did, he felt a stab of grief and a watering of his eyes. But the pain in Mrs. Reilly's eyes was something he had never seen before. He feared that her grief was so intense that she would never be able to live her life out in peace.

"Of course you can come back to work. But promise me that if you ever need to take off or need anything, you will tell me," Jacob said.

"But you have done so much already."

"Promise me, Mrs. Reilly."

"I promise," Mrs. Reilly finally said. "Thank you Jacob, Franklin." She paused. "Do you think I might have a word in private with you and Franklin?"

"Molly, would you mind putting on some tea for Mrs. Reilly? I'll send her to you in a few minutes and you can catch her up on what you have been doing," Jacob said.

"Of course," Molly replied as she left the room.

Mike got up to leave, but Mrs. Reilly motioned him to sit down as she composed her thoughts.

"Jacob, Molly is a sensible and nice girl and I did not want her to hear what I have to say," Mrs. Reilly started. "God forgive me, but I want the people who did this to Sean to be punished. I am a god fearing Catholic and I may go to hell, but I want them punished." She began to cry.

Mike was the first to speak. "Ye have heard that it hath been said, an eye for an eye, and a tooth for a tooth. Matthew 5:38."

Both Jacob and Franklin looked at Mike in stunned amazement.

Mike said, "Altar boy."

"Mrs. Reilly, I promise in a couple of weeks the people who did this will never be able to do it again. Now please go have some tea with Molly. She has missed you. We all have," Jacob said as he kissed her forehead.

"Thank you, Jacob. Thank you." Jacob gave her a hug. "Thank you, Franklin. Thank you, Mike."

"Mrs. Reilly, could you ask Molly to come in? I promise I'll send her back in just a couple of minutes," Jacob asked.

"Surely," Mrs. Reilly said and left the room.

In a few minutes, Molly entered. "You wanted me Jacob?"

"Yes, please sit." Jacob gestured to the seat next to him. "Mrs. Reilly is coming back to work and I would like you to work with her for a couple of weeks. Keep an eye on her. Can you do that for me?"

"Yes, of course. When she's back on her feet I'll find some place to stay."

Jacob's heart seemed to skip a beat. "Why? Uh, don't you like it here?"

"Oh yes, of course I do; but with Mrs. Reilly back you won't be needing me," Molly answered.

"Well, yes I do. I mean we do. Right, Frank?" Jacob stammered.

"Yeah, sure. We need you here," Franklin said in an assuring manner.

"But what would I do? Mrs. Reilly is more than capable to handle the house affairs." Molly knew she was goading Jacob a little, but she couldn't help herself.

"Um, well…Mike, is the corner store still vacant?"

"Yep," Mike answered.

"Well, that's it. I've wanted to rent that to someone ever since Mrs. Scott passed away. The street's not the same without a candy store," Jacob said more assuredly.

"I can't afford to rent a store!" Molly exclaimed.

"No, No. I'll open the store and you run it for me. You can get Jimmy to help you after school. It will be good for him. You can sell sodas, candy, cigarettes and stuff like that. We can even rent out the apartment upstairs. What do you say?" Jacob asked.

"Wouldn't I stay in the apartment?" Molly asked.

"Well… no. You see, I have become very attached to Jimmy and it would sadden me to see him leave, even if it was just down the street," Jacob lied. Jacob was attached to Jimmy, but it was Molly he was falling for and he wanted her close. The thought of her leaving gave him a pain in the pit of his stomach.

"Well…. Okay then. I'll take you up on your offer. It sounds like fun and I can be of use as well," Molly said.

"Great. Then shake to seal the deal," Jacob said.

Molly put out her hand and grasped Jacob's and shook. Then she kissed him on the cheek and almost danced out of the room. Jacob turned scarlet red.

"Don't! Don't you two say a word. Not a fucking word."

Franklin and Mike both looked at Jacob and shrugged their shoulders.

During the week that followed, Jacob, Franklin and Mike finished their planning. Their strategy was to first take out Mahoney and Colin McCurdy. Both were in Atlantic City together. Then he would reason with the rest of the Mahoney crew that it would be in their best interest to allow Jacob and Franklin to take over, including the large speakeasy and breweries on Girard Avenue. Jacob and his father had the political connections to make that a smooth transition.

As for Sal Sansone, that would be a different story. The Italians had a code they followed and killing their boss would cause an all out war. That is, unless Jacob was able to reason with Sal's replacement, who they thought would be Gerardo Amato. The one thing the Italians liked more than their code was cash. The idea was to take out Sansone and ask for a meeting with Amato. During the meeting, they would offer to give them a piece of the Mahoney action and supply their South Philly speakeasies with beer at a discounted rate. That still left Jacob's crew with a large increase in revenue and there would be peace between North and South Philly. Peace was always preferable for making money. It was risky, but Jacob thought it could work.

Mahoney and Sansone would have to be dealt with on the same night. Once Sansone got word of the Mahoney hit he would go into hiding and it would be very difficult to get to him. Jacob, Franklin, Mike and another of the crew would first travel to Atlantic City. Their sources had pinpointed where Mahoney and his second in command were holding up—they were in a friend's house near the beach. It should be easy to approach the house, do the job and then make the three-hour drive back to Philly and take care of Sansone before he heard any news.

Sansone had a habit of having breakfast at a little restaurant located on Washington Avenue near Eighth Street every morning at 7AM. They would hit him when he came out.

"Everything ready?" Jacob asked.

"Everything is good. Stop worrying," Franklin replied.

"I'm not fucking worrying. I like to be prepared. This is no easy thing. We need to get to Atlantic City, take care of that prick Mahoney and get back in time to hit Sansone at breakfast," Jacob said.

"Okay, okay; simmer down. We'll do it," Franklin said as he opened the door to the Packard.

"Mike, you drive the Ford truck. Whitey's with you. Frank and me will take the Packard. Just follow. We'll take the ferry over and then the Blackhorse to AC," Jacob said.

"Got it," Mike replied.

The Packard's twin V12 engine roared to life as Jacob hit the starter. He loved his Packard. It was sleek, durable and the engine was superb. He had seen President Warren Harding riding in a Packard when he was inaugurated in 1921, and Jacob had made a vow that he would own a Packard one day. As soon as he had the money, he bought the royal blue Packard. It was always a pleasure to drive, and it was fast. It could go up to seventy miles per hour, although Jacob had never pushed it that hard.

"Jakey, what's the deal with you and Molly?" Franklin asked.

"Frank... come on. 'Jakey'? What the fuck," Jacob said.

"You look like a Jakey tonight. What can I say? We were talking about Molly," Franklin said laughing.

"And you look like an asshole," Jacob replied.

"Come on. Molly?" Franklin insisted.

"Be serious for a minute?" Jacob asked.

"Okay," Franklin said as he pretended to wipe the smile off his face.

"Well, I like her. She is pretty and smart. And I like the kid," Jacob said.

"And that body—whew!" Franklin said.

"Am I going to have to shoot you before we get to AC?" Jacob asked.

"Okay, okay. Go on."

"That's it," Jacob said.

"Well what are you going to do about it? The girl obviously likes you. Otherwise she would be all over me," Franklin said.

"Oh boy!" Jacob exclaimed in fake frustration. "I guess I'll marry her someday."

"What? Are you fucking nuts? Marry! Why buy the cow when you can get the milk for free?" Franklin said.

"Frank, I'm not you. I don't want to go around fucking every girl I meet. I want a family, with kids, you know?" Jacob said.

"First of all, I don't fuck every girl I meet. They have to be cute, have a great body, and preferably be married. Secondly, I really don't know, but I guess if you have to get married, Molly would be a good one," Franklin said.

"I am glad you agree. I thought I would have to get somebody else to be Best Man," Jacob said.

"Yeah, and if you do I'll beat your ass all over Allegheny Avenue," Franklin said as he lightly smacked the back of Jacob's head.

The trip to Atlantic City was uneventful. The roads were not the best, but they worked fine for thousands of people who used them to get to Atlantic City in the summer. There wasn't a lot of traffic, now that the summer crunch had passed. Franklin and Jacob continued their good-natured ribbing. It eased the tension.

When they arrived in Atlantic City, it was late evening. They headed to the house where the informer said they would find Mahoney.

"I don't see any cars," Franklin said.

"Maybe they're out on the town. We'll park down the road where they can't see us and wait," Jacob said. "Go tell Mike, will you?"

Waiting was something that annoyed Jacob. He hated lines and he didn't like sitting around. When he had work to do, he wanted to do it and get it over with. It made him nervous not to be doing something. He wasn't sure why he was this way, but he probably got it from his father, who was a notoriously impatient man. Once, his father promised to take him to a Phillies game and was supposed to pick him up from school at 3 PM. Jacob's teacher delayed him for five minutes to discuss a paper he had handed in. By the time Jacob was done, his father had left and gone to the game without him. When Jacob asked why, the old man just said, "Never be late again. There are consequences for being late."

"That fucking bastard," Jacob thought.

"Yo! Wake up, fuck head!!" Franklin yelled.

Jacob grabbed for his pistol. "Jesus Christ, Frank! What the fuck? You scared the shit out of me. You're lucky I didn't blow your overused balls off."

"Take it easy. Just trying to get the juices going," Frank replied, laughing.

Jacob drove the car to a safe place past the driveway. It was another two hours before they saw two sets of headlights coming down the road and then turning into the driveway.

"Okay. This is it," Jacob said. "You ready, Frank?"

"Ready."

Jacob heard the doors close.

"Give it ten minutes. Let them get settled and then we go," Jacob said.

It was a long ten minutes and Jacob and Franklin used the time to discuss how they would approach the house.

Let's go," Jacob said.

When they got out of the car, Mike and Whitey ran up. Everyone knew the plan and what they had to do. Mike motioned for Whitey to follow him as he ran in a crouch to the beach and into his designated position. Frank and Jacob moved towards the front of the house.

"Ahhh fuck!" Franklin said in a whisper.

"What is it?" Jacob said.

"It's starting to rain."

"So? Afraid you'll melt?"

"I just bought this hat for five bucks and now it's fucked," Frank whispered with irritation.

"Are you fucking kidding me? You can buy a thousand hats when we take over Mahoney's gang," Jacob said.

Franklin shrugged.

The guard in the front had moved under the eave at the door. It was a cold rain and the man was hunched over with his hands in his pockets. Jacob motioned Franklin to one side of the eave and he took position on the opposite side. They inched their way to the man.

Jacob put his gun to the man's head, grabbed his pocketed hand, and said. "Be quiet and I won't blow your head off."

The guard made a slight move to his left and Franklin put his gun to the man's head and said, "Don't do it. Be calm and you live."

"Frank, take him to the truck," Jacob said.

Frank took the man's gun and whispered t o him, "Come on and be quiet," When they got to the truck, Franklin opened the back door and took out some rope and a gag. He put the gag in place and tied the man's hands behind him. He motioned the man to get in the truck. The man's eyes widened.

"Look; if you stay calm and quiet you have nothing to worry about. Now get in," Franklin said.

When the guard was in the truck, Franklin tied his feet, shut the door, and returned to Jacob who was crouching by the side of the door. The rain was coming down in buckets and both men were soaked.

Jacob looked through the window to see where Mahoney and McCurdy were. He could see McCurdy sitting by the fireplace, but Mahoney wasn't with him.

Mike and Whitey had positioned themselves on the side of the house close to the back door. Mahoney's second guard was just inside the doorway. They waited for Jacob and Franklin to make their move.

"I don't see Mahoney," Jacob whispered. "But McCurdy is here by the fireplace in the living room. Take a peek through your window."

Franklin stuck his head up and peered through the window.

"Well?" asked Jacob.

"Nothing. Just the dining room."

"Fuck! Where is he?" Jacob asked.

"Don't know, but we can't wait much longer," Franklin replied.

"Okay... I'll take McCurdy and you find Mahoney," Jacob said and both men kicked the door down. Jacob rushed at McCurdy, his gun in his hand. McCurdy jumped in surprise and grabbed for his gun on the table. Jacob shot three times, hitting McCurdy in the back and head. He fell hard, his right hand landing in the fireplace.

Mike and Pat, when they heard the first shoot, ran to the back door, kicked it in and Mike smashed his gun on the backdoor guard's head as he was getting up to respond to the shooting. He fell like a sack of potatoes.

"Stay here and watch him," Mike told Whitey as he ran into the kitchen. He saw a gun barrel poking out behind the door to the dining room and dove to the floor with his gun pointed at the door.

"Mike! It's me, Frank! You take the bedroom to the left and I'll do the other."

Mike ran to the bedroom and kicked open the door. He then took a crouching position, his gun pointed upward. No one was in the bedroom. He ran back to where Franklin was standing to the side of a bedroom door. Franklin gestured that Mike should stand on the other side of the door.

Jacob turned into the hallway, gun at the ready, and Franklin held his hand up for him to stay put. Jacob couched in the hallway.

"Okay fuck head, come out of there," Franklin yelled. Three shots rang out putting three neat holes high on the door where a man's chest would be. A second later, they heard a crash of glass and wood.

Franklin nodded to Mike, who smashed through the door ready to shoot.

"He went through the window," Mike yelled as he followed Mahoney through the broken pane.

"I'll take the back. You take the front," Jacob said as he motioned to Franklin. Both men took off running.

Jacob looked up and down the beach and saw two dark figures running south on the wet sand.

"Frank! He's on the beach!" Jacob yelled as he took off running. Three more shots rang out. He could hear Frank coming up behind him. He heard two more shots. The lights were coming on in several nearby homes.

"We need to hurry, Jacob. Cops will be here soon," Franklin said, panting.

As Jacob and Franklin caught up with the figures, they saw Mike standing over Mahoney who had fallen in the sand.

"Guys! What's this about?" Mahoney said in a fearful voice.

"It's about Sean Reilly, you cunt," Mike said as he shot at Mahoney's leg, shattering his knee.

Mahoney screamed in agonizing pain as the blood turned the sand red.

"It's also about Tim O'Hare," Franklin said as he shot Mahoney's other knee.

Mahoney screamed again as Jacob pointed his gun to his head and said, "And this is for Mrs. Reilly, you fuck!" He squeezed the trigger and blew off the top of Mahoney's head.

"Let's get out of here!" Franklin yelled.

As they were running back to the house, several people had come out to see what all the noise was. Mike fired several rounds into the air and they all went back to the safety of their homes. When they reached the cars, Whitey was already there and had put the second guard in the truck. They drove off and as Jacob looked back towards the house, he saw flames coming from the living room window.

The trip back to the ferry was uneventful. They arrived an hour before the ferry opened and took advantage of the time to rest. They checked on the two guards and assured them that if they were cooperative, they wouldn't be harmed. They agreed and Jacob had the ropes and gags removed.

"Guys, I'm sorry but when we get off the ferry we'll need to tie you up again. Just rest up and I'll see if I can get something to eat," Jacob said.

There were several other cars and a couple of fruit and vegetable wagons also waiting for the ferry. Farmers from New Jersey visited the city daily, traveling up and down the streets in their horse-drawn carts selling their harvests.

Jacob bought a couple bushels of apples. He opened the door to the truck and gave the men a couple apples each. He passed an apple to Mike, Whitey and one to Frank. Then he took a big bite of his own.

"There is nothing better than a Jersey apple," Jacob said.

"Except a Pennsylvania apple," Franklin said, smiling, as the farmer gave him a dirty look.

They waited another hour until the ferry was open, and loaded the cars. Once the ferry docked, they drove off to an isolated spot and discussed their plans again.

"The restaurant is close to the end of the block so Mike and Whitey will park the Packard around the block and be ready when Frank and I do the drive-by with the truck. You know what to do, Mike?" Jacob asked.

"Got it," Mike replied.

"Okay. Then let's go," Franklin ordered.

The men switched vehicles and drove to the restaurant where Sansone was supposed to be dining. Mike parked the Packard on the corner of Eighth and Ellsworth, and he and Whitey walked up to Eighth and Washington to buy some cakes at the corner bakery. They stood on the corner eating the cakes, and Jacob pulled the truck up to the middle of the block between Seventh and Eighth and waited.

Forty-five minutes later, Jacob saw Sansone and four bodyguards exit the restaurant. He started up Washington Avenue towards Eighth Street and when they were close to the group of men, Franklin and Jacob started shooting madly. They took the men by surprise and one man went down. The rest returned fire as the truck traveled west.

At exactly the same time, Mike and Whitey dropped the cakes, drew their weapons and ran up to where Sansone stood. Mike and Whitey opened fire as the men faced the truck. The three remaining bodyguards dropped as Sansone whirled around in surprise. At the same time, a bullet hit him in the chest and another in the neck. The blood spurted from the wound as he dropped to the ground and died.

Mike and Whitey ran back to the parked Packard and drove off. Jacob and Franklin continued up Washington and turned north on Tenth and back to North Philly. Both met back on Wishart Street.

"Bring these two in the house," Franklin said, motioning to the two Mahoney guards.

"Right," Mike said. Mike untied the guards and took them by the arm guiding, them to the house.

Mrs. Reilly had heard the cars and was waiting at the front door.

"Mrs. Reilly, we have guests for breakfast," Jacob said. "Take the guys to the dining room, will you Mike?"

"Let's go," Mike said as he guided the two men to the dining room.

"Mrs. Reilly, can we talk to you for a moment?" Jacob asked. Mrs. Reilly nodded silently. "Good. Then let's go to the living room."

"Please sit," Jacob gently commanded. Mrs. Reilly sat on the sofa as Jacob continued. "I want you to know that Sean has been avenged. That is all I can say for now, and I won't discuss the details. We can never talk about this again. Understand?" Jacob asked.

Mrs. Reilly crossed herself and said. "In the name of the Father, Son and Holy Ghost. Thank you, Jacob. Thank you, Franklin," she said, now sobbing heavily. She kissed each of them on the cheek as tears filled her eyes.

"Now let's get you some breakfast. You must be hungry."

After Mrs. Reilly brought the men coffee she started making a breakfast of eggs, bacon and fried potatoes.

Franklin and Jacob took their seats at the dining room table. Mike, Whitey and the two Mahoney men were already sitting.

"What're your names?" Franklin asked.

"Grady Hanlon."

"Brian Hanlon."

"What the fuck? You two are brothers?" Franklin asked, surprised.

"Yeah; same father, different mothers," Grady replied.

"Okay; Grady and Brian Hanlon—here's the deal. Your boss, Mahoney, is dead, along with that grease ball Sansone. And we're taking over. Nobody else has to die. This is a good deal for you and the rest of your crew. You're going to make more money than you ever thought you could. Every drop of beer, every sip of booze in North Philly will be supplied by us," Jacob explained.

"We need you to go to the others in your gang and explain this. Make them understand it's in their best interest to come in with us. If anyone causes trouble, they're dead. If anyone crosses us, they're dead. If anyone talks to the cops or the Italians, they're dead. Got it?" Franklin asked.

"Yeah. I'll try," Grady said.

"You need to do better than try, Grady. Brian will stay with us while you go talk to your guys. Make the case and you and Brian will get a bonus. If not...," Franklin said as he shrugged his shoulders.

"How many men in the gang, Grady?" Jacob asked.

" Eighteen, counting us," Grady said.

Jacob reached in his pocket and pulled out a wad of cash.

He counted out $5,500 dollars and handed it to Grady.

"Here's $250 for each of them and an extra $500 each for you and your bother. A little extra, because we had to rough you up a little. When you get an answer, come back and let me know."

Grady's eyes widened.

"And Grady. I don't have to tell you what will happen if that money doesn't get distributed fairly. You have twenty-four hours," Franklin said.

Grady looked at Franklin's stone cold face and then to Jacob. As he began to stand up, Jacob motioned him to sit. "Have some breakfast first. Mrs. Reilly is a great cook."

6

Grady Hanlon went straight to the Girard Avenue club, where he knew most of the men would be this time of day. Even though the temperature was cool, he was sweating. This would be no easy job. Not that the men cared that much about Mahoney. He was an ass and a cheap fuck at that. The guys would be more worried about their own skins and the money they might lose under a new boss.

Hanlon opened the club door and was greeted by a guard.

"Hiya Charlie," Hanlon said.

The guard tipped his hat and asked, "Morning. Where's the boss?"

"Lock the door and come on up to the bar. I have some news."

Grady made his way to the bar and shouted, "Yo! Listen up!"

After Grady had the men's attention, he said, "Mahoney and McCurdy are dead."

"What the fuck are you talking about? How? Who did it?" one of the men asked. The others were restless and murmuring to each other.

"Shut the fuck up," Grady yelled. "He's dead. The Front and Allegheny gang did it."

"Let's go. We'll kill all of those fuckers," another man said.

"Stop! Listen, this is a good thing for us," Grady said.

"How's that? We're next," another said.

"They want us to join them."

"What the fuck? They kill our boss and want us to join them? Fuck them. We'll join them in hell."

"Take it easy. What the fuck was Mahoney to any of us? He was a fucking prick and a cheap fuck. How many of you have two bucks in your pocket? He kept everything except what he paid the Italians. He was a fucking coward who bent over for Sansone," Grady said.

The men were murmuring again.

"And these fucking F and A guys are better?" a man asked.

"Yeah they are. First, they could have laid me and Brian out, but they didn't. They're not after us, they wanted Mahoney. He's the one who agreed to hit them for fucking Sansone. And who got dead? Our guys, not the Italians. Fuck Mahoney and fuck the Italians," Grady said.

More murmuring.

"What about Sansone? He ain't going to like this," someone said.

"Dead," Grady said.

"What?" The crowd was much louder now. "These F and A guys did that too?" someone asked.

"Yeah," Grady said as he wiped his brow. "Look, these guys, Jacob and Frank, are okay. I'm telling you we're going to make a lot more money and we won't be bending over for the Italians no more. These guys are taking over all of North Philly and I know they can do it."

Grady paused to let it sink in. "I want to be a part of that. That's where the money will be. What about you guys?"

The men talked to each other and Grady felt it was going pretty well. If it didn't, Brian was dead and so was he. Grady pulled out a wad of cash and threw it on the table.

"Here! Jacob sent a signing bonus. Two-fifty for each of us. I took mine and Brian's already. He told me there would plenty more where that came from. Dig in."

7

Two hours later, Grady rang the bell at 125 Wishart. Mrs. Reilly answered. "Oh, Mr. Hanlon, good afternoon."

"Afternoon, Miss. I'm here to see Jacob and Frank," Grady replied.

"I know, Mr. Hanlon. They've been waiting for you. Come in. Wipe your feet, mind you," Mrs. Reilly said. "Mr. Mike wants to see you first."

"Mike! It's Mr. Hanlon."

Mike nodded to Grady and held his arms up in a gesture that meant Grady should do the same. Grady complied and Mike frisked him.

"I'm not stupid, Mike," Grady said.

"Can't be too careful, Grady. Something for you to keep in mind," Mike said and he showed him into the dining room.

Brian Hanlon was sitting at the large table with Jacob on one side and Franklin on the other. In front of him was a large roast beef sandwich made with a German Kaiser roll, and a Hires Root Beer. Jacob and Frank had the same. Jacob looked at Mike who nodded.

Jacob rose from his chair and placed the .38 Revolver he had on his lap on the table.

"Grady, you're just in time. Sit down and have some lunch," Jacob said.

"Thanks," Grady replied as he took a chair across from Jacob.

"Mike," Jacob said as he motioned for Mike to sit. Mike sat next to Grady.

Mrs. Reilly brought a tray with sandwiches and sodas for Grady and Mike. "Eat up boys, I have more in the kitchen," she said.

Franklin reached for the horseradish, handed it to Grady and said. "Grady, try some horseradish on your sandwich. It's freshly ground this morning. Guy comes around every day."

"Thanks," Grady said tentatively, not knowing what to expect from Jacob and Franklin. He put the horseradish on his roast beef and took a bite.

"There. What did I tell you? Great, huh? Mrs. Reilly slices the beef very thin. It makes for a better sandwich," Franklin said.

"Yeah," Grady replied.

The five men sat in silence, finishing their sandwiches and sodas. It was obvious that Grady was ill at ease and Jacob wondered if the news he bore was bad. He didn't want to kill Brian and Grady. They seemed like good guys, but if the Front and Girard guys didn't want to join him he would have no alternative.

"So," Jacob said. "What's the news?"

"I told the guys we would be better off working with you and I gave them the money," Grady said.

"But?" Franklin asked.

"No, no. They were grateful for the money and want to consider it," Grady said.

"But?" Franklin asked again.

"But they want to meet with you and Jacob first," Grady said.

" A sit down?" Jacob asked.

"Yeah," Grady said.

Jacob stared at Grady for a long time. This heightened Grady's anxiety. "Well, let's do it then," Jacob said. "We'll meet on the corner of the new Frankford Elevated station at Kensington and Allegheny. Our guys and your guys. No guns, Grady. You hear me? Make it three o'clock."

"Yes boss," Grady said, wanting to show Jacob that he was committed.

"Call me Jacob. Now take Brian and go home. Your families must be worried."

Grady and Brian left, but not before Mrs. Reilly presented them with a bag of several more roast beef sandwiches to take with them.

After Grady and Brian left, Jacob, Franklin and Mike looked at each other in silence for a moment. Jacob pursed his lips and blew out in relief.

"Now what?" Mike asked.

"Get four of your best shooters. Two on the El platform and two inside the station. Give them rifles, not Thompsons. If trouble starts I don't want them spraying all of us with lead," Jacob said. "Get eighteen of our guys together and fill them in. I want to have as many men as they have. And tell them I don't want any guns showing."

"I'll have them ready outside at two-thirty," Mike said.

"No. Have them walk over in small groups. I don't want to attract too much attention. Just be sure they're all there by two-forty-five. They can hang out on the corner near the bank," Jacob said.

At 2:50 PM Jacob and Franklin told Mrs. Reilly they would be back before dinner and started the ride over to Kensington and Allegheny Avenue. There was a car in front of them and one behind, both with well-armed men. The Italians had not reacted yet, but they would and Jacob was sure of that.

The Italians loved a large funeral and always made a spectacle when one of the bosses died. Jacob was hoping this would keep them busy until after he sealed the deal with the Front and Girard guys.

As they traveled East on Allegheny Avenue, Jacob couldn't help feeling a sense of pride at the homes and business he saw. The Wishart Theater was particularly beautiful, with its bright marquee and all-glass doors. His father, Franklin, and he had a lot to do with how attractive this area had become. Yes, it was a working man's neighborhood, but the people living here cared for their homes. It was normal to see the ladies of the houses sweeping the sidewalks and picking up trash thrown from people in the cars and the Trolley. Jacob wondered if all this would still be here in a hundred years and what it would be like. He hoped it kept its charm.

"You strapped?" Franklin asked.

"Yeah—in my boot," Jacob answered.

"Me too."

The cars pulled up to the northeast corner at Kensington and Allegheny in front of the Frankford Elevated building. Jacob saw that both crews were there. Most of Jacob's men were in front of the bank, and the Girard Avenue guys were on the Kensington Avenue side of the building. As he and Franklin were getting out of the car, Grady, Brian and Mike walked over.

"Jacob, Frank," Grady said as he shook each man's hand.

"How we doing, Grady? The guys going to play ball?" Jacob asked.

"Let's go meet them," Grady said.

Grady introduced Jacob, Franklin and Mike to each man and Jacob and Franklin answered their questions. When they were done the Girard Avenue guys all agreed to be part of Jacob and Franklin's gang.

"Grady, you did a great job. I appreciate it," Jacob said.

Grady nodded his head and smiled. He said, "I guess we need a new name for the gang now."

"He's right, Jacob," Franklin said.

"Have anything in mind, Grady?" Jacob asked.

"How about the Byrne's Gang?" Grady asked.

"No… I don't think so, Grady. I am not looking to advertise myself," Jacob said.

"How about we name it after here?" Brian said.

"What the fuck is here? Shut your pie hole, Brian," Grady said.

"No, asshole. I mean here," Brian said waving his arms around. "We can be the 'K and A gang.'"

They all paused for a few seconds and Jacob said, "Okay Brian. From now on we're the 'K and A Gang.'" Jacob put his arm around Brian. "Let's all go over to Jack's Place. I am buying. They have the best whiskey. I should know. We sell it to them."

As both crews, now united, started walking to Jack's, Jacob put his other arm around Grady and said, "Grady you're the boss of your old crew and Brian's your second. The Girard Avenue place is your headquarters and you report directly to Frank or me."

Franklin took Grady's hand and shook it. "Congratulations."

Grady looked surprised and then smiled.

8

The Italian mob was distracted by the death of Sansone, and infighting between three of Sansone's chiefs—Gerardo Amato, Franky Capaci and Carlo Manganella—was really slowing business down. Franky Capaci was the youngest of the three and thought Amato and Manganella were old fashioned, old-country buffoons who didn't know the modern, American way to conduct a sound operation. Amato had the support of the soldiers in the field, but decided to allow Capaci the top post to avoid conflict. He felt Capaci would soon burn himself out with his impetuous ways and then he would take over. Manganella was furious and threatened Capaci and Amato with an all out internal war.

On the Sunday morning after Sansone was buried, Maganella and his family attended Mass at St. Nicholas, a popular South Philly church where the priest spoke Italian. This was a weekly ritual, routine as clockwork. When Mass had adjourned, Maganella met with the Priest on the church steps and handed him an envelope with a generous donation. Maganella always made his donation in person and in public because he wanted to be sure everyone knew where the money came from. He hoped that his generosity would open the gates of Heaven and the community.

As he walked down the stairs of the church to the sidewalk, his wife and two sons behind him, a car stopped at the curb. Four shots rang out and Manganella dropped to the sidewalk, bleeding from his chest. He died instantly. The car slowly drove off as Manganella's wife stood screaming on the church steps. With his death, Capaci was catapulted to the top of the South Philly Italian mob, and his first order of action was to eradicate the "K and A Gang.'"

Franky Capaci was in his early thirties and tall for an Italian. He had unusual blue eyes and scar on his right hand where someone had sliced him in a knife fight. His appearance was menacing and it matched his personality.

"Look Gerardo, I don't give a fuck about Sansone, Maganella, or any other fuck who gets in my way. I want North Philly. And if we gotta kill every fucking Mick gangster in North Philly to get it, then so be it," Capaci said.

"I'm just saying. You know? A war will cut into our business. We won't be making money. Maybe we should wait a while," Amato said.

"No! And fuck no. Our guys are worked up now. They're pissed the Micks killed Sansone. Now's the time to hit 'em," Capaci said, banging his fist on the table.

When Amato heard Capaci mention Sansone, he made the sign of the cross.

"You fucking old country guys and your religion," Capaci blurted out. "What the fuck? He's dead. And if he's anywhere, he's in Hell and someday we'll meet him there. But not today, and not soon. Fucking Moustache Petes."

Amato crossed himself again.

"Awww fuck! Look, I need to hit now while the iron's hot. The guys want revenge, I want North Philly," Capaci said.

"But I..." started Arnato.

"But fucking nothing. If you don't like it maybe I can arrange your retirement," Capaci yelled.

Amato's face showed a hint of fear, but inside he was smiling. Capaci, the fucking ignorant shit that he was, was doing exactly what he wanted. A war with the North Philly gang would make it very hard for his soldiers to make money. Once their revenge-lust was used up, they would be looking at why they were broke and it would be Capaci they were looking at. At the right time, he would hand over or kill Capaci himself and make the peace. Once Capaci was gone, Amato would take charge and the guys would be happy to get back to making money.

"No!" Amato said, putting his hands up in a sign of surrender. "You're the boss. How do you want to do it?"

"We need a hard hit. Something big. Something they will notice. We can't get at Byrne and Garrett while they're in the house. They got that place shut up tighter than a Nun's twat," Capaci said.

Amato made the sign of the cross.

"Jesus fucking Christ. Stop this bullshit," Capaci said as he mockingly made the sign of the cross in the air. "Give me some fucking ideas."

"How about we take out the old man?"

"What the fuck are you talking about? What old man?" Capaci asked.

"Byrne's father. The moneyman. That should get the kid's attention. Might even get him out of his compound," Amato said. He was hoping Capaci would go for this. If he ordered that hit, the younger Byrne would hit back hard and the war would be bloody. The kid would also inherit the old man's money and construction company. That would be good for when things calmed down and he could strike a deal with the younger Byrne, if he were still alive in the aftermath.

Capaci sat staring at Amato for several minutes, then said, "Okay. Let's do it. Get the fuck out and send **Pascucci** in to see me."

"What, you don't want me to do it?" Amato asked with a feigned incredulity.

"Fuck no. You send some guys over to Kensington and kill a couple Micks. That'll keep them busy while we're working on getting the old man. I'll take care of that. And cut off that fucking moustache," Capaci said.

Amato left the room thinking that things were progressing quickly and progressing well. Capaci was arrogant and stupid, he thought. He, Amato, had killed his first man when he was fourteen, and plenty more since. And he would kill Capaci when the right time came.

The integration of the Girard Avenue boys with the Front and Allegheny gang was going well. Everyone was interested in making money, so working together got them all what they wanted. The only cloud in this otherwise silver lining was the Italians. Everyone knew they would hit, they just didn't know when or where. The Wishart Street headquarters and the Girard Avenue place were buttoned down, and Jacob had ordered his various speakeasies to be on the alert.

"Any word from our man down south?" Jacob asked Franklin.

"No. Nothing. With the regime change he is not close to the top anymore," Franklin said.

"Fuck! I wish these cock suckers would get on with it. I hate waiting. Maybe we should hit first," Jacob said.

"No, I don't think that's a good idea. We still don't know who's going to land on top. If it's Amato we might be able to have a meeting to iron things out. If it's someone else, I don't know," Franklin said.

Mrs. Reilly entered the room and cleared her throat.

"You need something Mrs. Reilly?" Jacob asked.

"Jacob, your father's man, Mr. Graham, is here to see you."

"Really? Okay, show him in, Mrs. Reilly," Jacob said tentatively. When Mrs. Reilly left the room, Jacob said, "What the fuck could he want?"

"Don't know, but I can tell you that guy still scares me after all these years," Franklin replied.

"I know what you mean," Jacob said.

Graham entered the room and followed Mrs. Reilly. "Please sit, Mr. Graham. May I get you something?"

"Thank you, no," Graham replied.

Both Jacob and Franklin shook Graham's hand. Jacob said, "This is a surprise. I don't believe you or my father have ever been here before."

"Never needed to be," Graham said.

"No, I guess not. What brings you here now?"

"Your father would like you and Mr. Garrett to come to dinner tonight at seven."

"So your telephones are all broke at the house?" Jacob asked.

"Your father doesn't like to discuss business on the telephone," Graham said.

"Since when?"

"Since now. Be there at seven," Graham said as he rose to leave. "Bring Mike with you."

Graham left the room with Jacob and Garrett following and Mrs. Reilly opened the door for him and said, "Good afternoon, Mr. Graham."

Graham bowed slightly, smiled and said, "Good afternoon, Mrs. Reilly." His car was parked in front of the house and he opened the door, turned around and tipped his hat to Mrs. Reilly and drove off.

"Mr. Graham is quite the dashing man, isn't he?" Mrs. Reilly asked, looking after the car as it drove down the street.

Jacob and Garrett looked at each other and laughed. Mrs. Reilly shook her head and left the room in a huff saying, "Oh, you two are incorrigible."

Mike, Franklin and Jacob drove to the Byrne Mansion in one car and were accompanied by four other cars—two in front, two behind. When they arrived, two cars took position at the rear of the house and two stood guard at the front. Jacob knocked on the door, and his father answered.

"Jacob. Thanks for coming," Byrne said as he grasped Jacob by the shoulder. "Garrett. Kelly," Byrne said as he shook each man's hand. "Come in. George has whipped up a fine meal for us."

Byrne led the three men to the spacious dining room. The table was set for six people.

"Can I get you a drink?" Byrne asked.

"Whiskey," Jacob replied.

"Me too," Garrett added.

"None for me sir," Mike said.

"None? You too good to drink with us, Mike?" Byrne asked.

"No sir, just..." Jacob interrupted Mike and said, "Mike'll have a whiskey."

"Good." Byrne poured five whiskies, handed each man a glass and put the fifth at the seat next to the head of the table.

"Where's Mr. Graham?" Garrett asked.

"He's in the kitchen cooking. Bet you didn't know that George was an excellent cook."

"No, I didn't," Franklin replied.

"Oh yeah. He's made a wonderful roast beef with gravy, cabbage and bacon, like from the old country. And of course, mashed potatoes. George has his own recipe for Soda bread. Wait till you taste it," Byrne said.

"Can't wait," Franklin said, a little too sarcastically.

"Have a seat and I'll go see what's keeping George," Byrne said.

When Byrne left the room, Franklin asked Jacob, "What the fuck is he up to?"

"I don't know, but he wants something," Jacob said.

"Are you kidding me? Graham cooks?" Franklin asked.

"Yeah, he often made our meals when I was a kid. He's a very good cook," Jacob said. "Let's sit. Frank you're next to me. Mike, take the seat across from Frank," Jacob said as he took his usual chair to the right of the head of the table.

Byrne came back into the dining room and took his seat at the head of the table. Graham was behind him carrying a large platter of thinly sliced roast beef. He placed the beef on the center of the table, left and ret urned with a large bowl of cabbage, mashed potatoes and a bowl of carrots and onions. One more trip to the kitchen and Graham placed two loaves of unsliced warm soda bread on the table.

"Dig in boys," Byrne said.

"Are we waiting for someone else, Mr. Byrne?" Franklin asked, pointing to the empty chair and place setting.

Jacob looked at his father and for a split second, a shadow of sadness passed over Byrne's face.

"No Frank. That's my mom's chair. Ever since Mom passed, my father has a place set for her every meal," Jacob explained.

"I'm sorry... I didn't..." Franklin started.

Byrne interrupted. "No, it's okay, Garrett. It is our way of honoring a very special woman. Let's eat, shall we?"

Mike and Graham made the sign of the cross and then ate.

"George, this beef is amazing. I've missed it," Jacob said. Graham nodded his head.

"You know all of this; everything I've done has been for Jacob. It'll all be his one day. Hopefully, a long time from now," Byrne said with a chuckle.

Jacob choked on a piece of beef.

"You okay, Jacob?" Byrne asked.

"Yeah... yes," Jacob replied hoarsely.

"As I was saying, we all have done well with our construction business. We can be proud of the contribution we have made to Philadelphia," Byrne continued.

Jacob had never heard his father use "we" when he was praising his own work. Normally it was "I made a great contribution to Philadelphia." His father must really want something important from him. What could he give his father that he didn't already have or couldn't do himself?

"Why did you invite all of us here, Father? What is it you want?" Jacob asked.

"I do have a small favor to ask, but that can wait until we have finished dinner. Please eat up. We don't want to disappoint George," Byrne said.

Graham glanced at Garrett who quickly started eating.

The rest of dinner was pleasant enough. Jacob's father was an avid baseball fan and loved the Phillies and he voiced his displeasure that they had only achieved eighth place in the National League that year. He spoke of the days, back in '88, when the team was the Philadelphia Quakers and they had taken second in the league. He claimed that the best players in the league at that time were Deacon McGuire, Ben Sanders and a Billy Hallman. The older Byrne had seen every home game that year at the Bakers Bowl located at Fifteenth Street and Lehigh Avenue.

"That's a ball field," Byrne claimed. "Not like that steel and concrete shithole Shibe Park the A's play in." He also didn't think football would last. "America's about baseball, not some overgrown goons running up and down a field with a funny looking ball."

Despite the unusual pleasantries coming from his father (or perhaps, because of them), Jacob felt uneasy. The old man wanted something and that something probably would not be good for Jacob.

"Ahh. Here's George with dessert. Bassett's Ice Cream. You remember Bassett's, don't you Jacob?" Byrne asked.

"Oh yeah! How could I forget? You have it every night after dinner. What I remember most is it was always Rum Raisin and I hated it," Jacob said.

"I know. You like Vanilla," Byrne said in feigned sadness.

"So why didn't you ever buy Vanilla?"

"Guess what? Tonight we have Vanilla. Just for you."

Jacob's stomach tightened. The old man was going all out to please him. This was going to be bad, very bad. Byrne was so transparent in his attempt to manipulate, Jacob almost laughed.

The men finished their dessert and retired to the living room to have coffee and after-dinner drinks. After Byrne poured the drinks, Graham gave a last minute instruction to the maid that they not be disturbed. He then shut the doors.

"Father, we appreciate the dinner and the ice cream, but you asked us here to discuss something. So I would appreciate it if you would stop stalling and ask what you want," Jacob said.

Byrne's face flushed and Jacob wasn't sure whether it was from anger or shame in asking his son a favor.

"Okay Jacob, here it is. As you know, I supplied weapons to the Cuban rebels before and during the Spanish-American War. And..." Jacob interrupted and said "And you supplied arms to the Spanish."

"Yes that's true. There were other certain customers who, let's say, were unsavory. If any of this became public now, I would lose my building contracts, maybe worse. It would be devastating to me and to you."

"I'm not going to tell anyone. How about you, George? You gonna tell?" Jacob asked sarcastically.

Byrne ignored Jacob's comments and said, "Two weeks ago the mayor announced the appointment of a new police commissioner—retired Admiral Henry Bannister."

"Yeah, we heard about that. Some bullshit about cleaning up the city. So what? That's just political talk. It's an election year," Jacob said.

"Two days ago I got a call from Bannister, and..."

Jacob interrupted. "You know him?"

"Yes and if you stop interrupting I can get through this more quickly." Jacob shrugged and Byrne continued. "As I was saying, Bannister called me and in no uncertain terms blackmailed me. He wants money. A lot of money. If he doesn't get it he'll talk about my past. He said he might even arrest me."

Jacob sat up straighter and leaned forward. "How does he know about your past?"

"Bannister was stationed in Miami and was the officer in charge of operations in that area. He arranged to get my weapons to Cuba. The son of a bitch made a fortune from me."

"Wait a minute. You're telling me you used US Navy ships to deliver illegal weapons?" Jacob asked.

"Yes. That's what I am saying."

"So what's the problem? If he arrests you, he incriminates himself. He won't do it," Jacob said.

"Jacob, you have a lot to learn. The fucker is a retired admiral and will be police commissioner. Who are they going to believe, me or him? No... I'm afraid I can't take that chance," Byrne said.

"What do you want us to do?" Jacob asked.

Byrne looked at Jacob, his eyes burrowed deep under his brows, and a slight smile curled in his cheeks.

"Kill the motherfucker."

Jacob, Garrett and Mike looked at each other in surprise. "Mr. Byrne, we can't kill a police commissioner. The whole department will come down on us like a ton of bricks. You'll lose your connections. It can't be done," Franklin said.

"Frank's right. It can't be done," Jacob said.

"Why not? He's not commissioner yet. He won't be for another couple of weeks. Listen..."

Jacob interrupted. "No, absolutely not. It can't be done."

"Listen to me!" Byrne yelled. "Bannister has a boat he keeps on the Chesapeake. He has a house nearby and he loves to sail. Sailing can be dangerous, you know. You can hit your head, fall overboard, whatever."

"So why do you need us? George is capable."

" No. It cannot be anyone close to me. I can't take that risk."

"For Christ's sake, Frank and I are pretty close," Jacob said.

"But Mike isn't," Byrne said.

Everyone looked at Mike.

"No... I don't know... This seems too dangerous. Killing such a big wig," Jacob said.

"Jacob I know what you three did to Mahoney and Sansone. So don't give me any shit. I know you can plan this and Mike can make it happen."

"Let's say we do it. What's in it for us? And don't say my inheritance."

"If you get this done you won't have to pay my share of your side business anymore," Byrne said. Jacob just looked at him. "And I'll give you twenty-thousand dollars."

Jacob wasn't quite satisfied.

"In addition to that, I want a list of all the politicians and cops you have on your payroll. I want you to introduce me to them."

"Okay I get it, Jacob. You want to make your own mark. I understand that, but that is too much," Byrne said.

"If you really believe what you said about doing all this for me then you shouldn't have a problem. Frankly, Father, you don't have a lot of options. I can do this for you and no one will ever know."

"You drive a very hard bargain, Jacob."

"I learned from the best, Father."

"Okay... deal," Byrne said.

"One more thing. Frank and I won't be coming to work anymore, but we'll still be on the payroll. If you need us to do you favors in the future we'll be there for you. Agreed?"

"Agreed," Byrne said as he slapped Jacob on the shoulder. "Let's have a drink."

"We'll pass on that, Father. Frank, Mike and I have some work to do.

"Oh Jacob, can you send over a couple cases of Cutty Sark over? I want to have a party in a few days. I'm hoping to celebrate," Byrne said.

"Sure," Jacob said, and then whispered to Franklin, "The old man always has to have the last word."

9

Molly Simms was enjoying her work at the candy store. It was fun and she felt a sense of accomplishment getting the store ready to open. She was sure that many of the neighborhood families would buy cigarettes, sodas, candy and especially ice cream. More than anything, Molly loved that Jimmy would be working with her at the store.

Living in Jacob's house was like getting a reprieve from Hell. Her mother-in-law had been a hard women and seemed to resent both Molly and Jimmy. Maybe they reminded her of her son. Molly didn't know. What she did know was it was much better now and she was falling in love with Jacob.

Each morning, Molly made Jimmy his lunch and sent him off to school. After Jimmy was gone she would have breakfast with Mrs. Reilly, Franklin and Jacob.

"Did you have a good dinner with your father last night, Jacob?" Molly asked.

"Yes, um, yes… it was good."

"Good," Molly said.

"Frank, would you and Mrs. Reilly find Mike for me and ask him to come see us?" Jacob asked.

"We don't need the both of us. Mrs. Reilly can…" Franklin began, but was cut off by Jacob, who was rolling his eyes toward Molly.

"Please!" Jacob insisted.

"Okay, Okay. Come on, Mrs. Reilly."

When they left the room, Jacob said, "Molly, I want you to know that I am well satisfied with your work in the store."

"Thank you, Jacob. That's nice of you to say."

"I have become very fond of you and Jimmy, you know. I was wondering if you, Jimmy and I could go on small trips together. You know, go see things, maybe a picture show or a museum. I want to get to know you both better," Jacob said.

"What about the store?"

"You're closed on Sundays, so we can go then."

"But we have church on Sunday," Molly said.

Jacob's mood saddened and he said, "Oh."

Molly interrupted him and said laughing, "Jacob, I'm joking. There is nothing more that I want than to spend time with you."

"Really?"

"Yes really," Molly said as she moved her lips close to Jacob's. "Don't you know that I love you?"

"And I love you, Molly." They kissed.

It seemed like they had kissed for a very long time before Molly broke it off and said, "Will you come to Mass with us on Sunday?"

"Oh, um, well… it's been so long. The church might fall down," Jacob said as he looked into Molly's soft brown eyes. "Yeah sure, I'll go to Mass." He kissed her again.

Franklin walked into the room, saw them kissing and turned around and walked out again.

"It's okay, Frank. You can come in," Jacob said.

"You two have a good discussion?" Franklin asked.

"Oh yes," Molly said, her face flushed.

"Mike's here, Jacob," Franklin said.

"Ask him to come in. Molly, could you give us a minute? I just need to talk to Mike," Jacob said.

"Sure, I'll go check on Mrs. Reilly."

"Thank you," Jacob said as he looked into Molly's eyes again.

"Jacob," Mike said and shook Jacob's hand.

"Hello Mike," Jacob said, not fully registering anything but the retreating beauty of Molly as she left the room. He shook Mike's hand limply, while still following Molly out the door with his eyes.

Franklin laughed until Jacob snapped out of it.

"The fucking Italians took out two of our guys last night," Mike said.

"Fuck!! Who?" Jacob asked, now serious.

"Two Girard Avenue guys. They were hanging out over at K and A. Three Italians in a car drove up and sprayed them. The guys are pissed. They want to hit back now," Mike said.

"No. Not yet," Jacob said. "When we hit them I want it to count and I want it hard."

"Okay Jacob, but we can't wait long," Mike said.

"I agree," Franklin said.

"We won't. I promise. Mike, would you get two, no, make it three cases of Cutty and take it over to my father's house? On the way back you can stop and see Grady. Tell him to get his guys ready and wait my word."

"Sure," Mike answered.

"Be careful. Take a few guys with you," Jacob said.

Mike nodded and left the room. Franklin looked at Jacob and raised his eyebrows.

"What?" Jacob asked.

"You know what."

"She told me she loved me," Jacob said.

"And what did you say?"

"I told her I loved her."

"Good—always tell them you love them. They like that," Franklin said.

"I do love her," Jacob said.

Franklin stared at him for a few seconds and said, "Can you stand now? We have work to do."

Mike put the three cases of Cutty Sark in the car and he and three others started to drive over to old man Byrne's house. Ten minutes after Mike drove off, a car pulled up and parked on Broad Street near Byrne's house. Two men dressed as telephone repairmen went to the back of the house and two others, also in uniform, knocked on the door. When the housekeeper opened the entrance, one of the men grabbed her, covering her mouth, as the other hit her over the head with the butt of his revolver.

The man laid her to the side of the door, being careful not to make too much noise. Then both men started searching for Byrne. Just as they reached his office door, George Graham started down the steps. He yelled, "What the fuck are you two doing?" as he pulled his pistol. The men turned, guns in hand, and fired. Graham was hit, and as he fell backwards, he squeezed his trigger. The shot went into the ceiling. The two men turned to open Byrne's office door, when two shots rang out from within. One of the men fell backwards, his face destroyed by a .45 caliber bullet.

The other man stepped to the side and threw the door open, crouching and diving into the room, shooting blindly in front of him. No one was in the room. Byrne had used a special door he had built that led to the house's back exit. As Byrne reached the back door, a man stood in front of the exit with a gun leveled at his chest. The man fired two shots, hitting Byrne at point blank range.

At the same time the assailant had shot Graham, Mike pulled up in front of Byrne's house. Hearing the first shots, he motioned two men to go to the back of the house and he and another one of his men burst through the door just as the assailant entered Byrne's office. Both Mike and his man shot the gunman, hitting him in the back of his head. He fell forward onto Byrne's desk.

Mike saw Graham lying on the steps and told his backup, "See how Graham is." Then he ran through the opened back office door. Just as he arrived, he heard several more shots ring out. Byrne was on the floor bleeding. The assailant who shot him was dead on the back step. One of Mike's men had come to the door and Mike quickly leveled the gun at him, but put it down just before squeezing the trigger.

"Is Byrne dead?" the man asked.

Mike kneeled next to Byrne and checked his pulse. "Not yet. Go call an ambulance. Phone's in the office," Mike said.

Mike's man came through the back office door and said, "Mike, Graham's shot but not dead. They got him in the shoulder. He's losing a lot of blood."

"How's the housekeeper?" Mike asked.

"Dead."

"Fuck," Mike said.

The phone rang at Jacob's house. Mrs. Reilly picked it up.

"Hello?"

"This is Mike. Get Jacob, will you!"

"What's wrong, Mike? You don't sound like yourself."

"Just get Jacob, please!"

Mrs. Reilly went to Jacob's office and told him Mike was on the phone. "He sounds nervous."

"My father probably gave him a hard time," Jacob said. "Don't worry about it."

Jacob picked up the phone. "Yeah?"

"The fucking Italians shot your father and Graham."

Jacob took a deep breath, his eyes wide. "Are they alive?"

"Yes… barely. I had the ambulance take them to the Pennsy. Jacob, he's shot bad," Mike said.

"How about Graham?"

"He's hit in the shoulder. Lost a lot of blood," Mike said.

"Meet me at the hospital and bring your men. I am leaving now," Jacob said.

Mrs. Reilly had heard Jacob's side of the conversation and asked, "What is it, Jacob? What's wrong?"

"They shot my father and George. Please get Frank and ask him to get four of the guys and meet me at Pennsylvania Hospital," Jacob said.

Mrs. Reilly made the sign of the cross and asked, "Are they alive?"

"Yes. I'll tell you more after I get to the hospital," Jacob said as he ran out of the room.

As Jacob drove to the hospital, he had a feeling of dread and regret. He had felt that way when his mother was ill. It puzzled him. He had been fighting with his father since he was a kid and the elder Byrne never seemed to be too interested in Jacob. Neither had they ever espoused any love for each other. When he was younger, Jacob had often wished his father would die. So why was Jacob shaking on the inside? Why was he so upset that his father actually might die… or even be dead now? Why hadn't he been nicer to his father? Why had he not told him he loved him? Now it might be too late.

When Jacob arrived at the hospital Mike was waiting outside for him.

"How is he?" Jacob asked

"They're working on him. No word yet. I have our men guarding the operating room and if… when… he gets out, we'll post them at his room," Mike explained.

"Frank's bringing more men. Have them look after the entrances and exits."

"Jacob, the hospital people are bitching at us and…"

Jacob interrupted. "I don't give a fuck. Pay them off. Do what you have to do. I'm not taking any chances. What about Graham?"

"Doc says he'll be okay. He's alive, but will be laid up for a while," Mike answered.

"Good. Okay, where's the operating room?"

After Mrs. Reilly told Frank to meet Jacob at the hospital, she went to the candy store to tell Molly what had happened.

"Oh no! What can we do to help?" Molly asked.

"Nothing yet. Jacob's going to call when he can."

"Who would do such a thing?" Molly asked.

"I don't know, but God knows Mr. Byrne has enemies."

"Let me close up here and I'll wait with you at the house," Molly said.

Molly and Mrs. Reilly returned to Jacob's house, brewed some tea and waited.

"Molly, let's say a Rosary for Mr. Byrne and Mr. Graham."

Mrs. Reilly and Molly took out their Rosary Beads and began the prayers. " I believe in God, the Father Almighty, Creator of heaven and earth; and in Jesus Christ, His only Son, our Lord; Who was conceived by the Holy Spirit, born of the Virgin Mary, suffered under Pontius Pilate, was crucified, died, and was buried. He descended into hell; the third day He arose again from the dead. He ascended into heaven, and sits at the right hand of God, the Father Almighty; from thence He shall come to judge the living and the dead. I believe in the Holy Spirit, the Holy Catholic Church, the communion of Saints, the forgiveness of sins, the resurrection of the body and life everlasting. Amen." When they finished, they said a special prayer that Mr. Byrne and Mr. Graham be brought back to good health.

"Molly, I know you and Jacob are becoming close and I think it is wonderful," Mrs. Reilly said.

"Thank you, Mrs. Reilly. I am very fond of him. Jimmy is also," Molly said.

"And he of you, both of you. I can assure you of that. Molly, you've been around long enough to know that Jacob's business is not just building houses. I want to be sure you know what becoming part of this family means," Mrs. Reilly said.

"Yes. I know," Molly said.

"There will be many secrets; things Jacob will not tell you. It will be for your own protection but you will always have doubts. Jacob's a good man and you have to understand that even good men must sometimes do bad things to protect their family," Mrs. Reilly said.

"I love Jacob and I will support him until I die," Molly said.

The phone rang. Mrs. Reilly rushed to answer it. When she finished the call, she made the sign of the cross and said, "Thank god, Mr. Graham is okay. He will recuperate in time."

"What about Mr. Byrne? Was that Jacob on the phone?" Molly asked frantically.

"It was Frank. Mr. Byrne is in worse shape, but the doctors think he'll survive. The bullets hit him in the chest, but by God's grace they missed his heart."

"Oh that is good news," Molly said.

"They think one of the bullets nicked Mr. Byrne's spine. He may not be able to walk."

"Oh no!"

"He's alive and that's a start. Praise God," Mrs. Reilly said.

"Yes, thank God."

"Frank asked if we could bring them some food. He has a lot of hungry men at the hospital," Mrs. Reilly said.

"I'll run down to the store and get some sodas to take with us," Molly said.

Jacob's father had come through the operation in as good a shape as could be expected. He was resting in his room. The doctor had told Jacob that there was a bullet still lodged near his spine. They couldn't take it out for fear it would damage the spine even more. The doctors didn't expect that Byrne would be able to walk and his recovery would be difficult. He would need constant care for at least a few months.

The doctors allowed Jacob to sit with his father. Byrne was still not conscious so Jacob just stared at his father and thought. He couldn't believe that this man, this vibrant strong man was now reduced to lying unconscious in a hospital bed. Jacob was confused. He was feeling fear, grief, pity, even love for a man he hadn't liked most of his life. Could you love someone you didn't like? Was the paternal link so strong that you could forgive your father for the cheating on your mother, the indifference and manipulation he had experienced?

Although Byrne was still unconscious, Jacob leaned in, kissed his forehead and said, "Dad, I love you." A single tear appeared in the older Byrne's eye and rolled down his cheek.

"How's your father, Jacob?" Frank asked as he closed the door behind him.

"He's holding his own," Jacob responded, wiping tears from his own eyes.

"We've got more problems. I'm sorry to bother you with this, but..."

Jacob interrupted him and said, "No it's okay. What is it?"

"Grady just got here and told me that the Italians hit several of our places near K and A. early this morning. No one was killed but they did a lot of damage. Grady's guys are pissed," Franklin said.

Jacob turned his head toward Franklin and stared at him, with a look that sent a shiver down Franklin's spine. He said, "How many men do we have now?"

"About ninety-five, give or take."

"Break them up into crews of ten and have each crew pick a leader. I want to meet with the leaders later tonight," Jacob said in a slow, cold voice.

"Okay. What do you have in mind?" Franklin asked.

"We are going to war. I told you a long time ago I would never let the Italians have North Philly. I meant it then and I mean it now. They have to pay for this," Jacob said, pointing to his father.

"Done," Franklin said.

Mrs. Reilly and Molly arrived at the hospital with bags of sandwiches and passed them out to the men. The nurses wouldn't let them see Byrne, so

Mrs. Reilly asked to see Graham. Graham was sitting propped up in his bed. His shoulder bone had been broken by the bullet and was in a cast.

"Good afternoon, Mr. Graham. How are you doing?" Mrs. Reilly asked.

"Okay," Graham replied.

"I've brought you a couple of sandwiches and a Pepsi Cola. You don't want to be eating this hospital food. You'll need your strength to recuperate."

"Thank you, Mrs. Reilly."

"Okay then, I'll be leaving. Take care," Mrs. Reilly said as she bent near and kissed Graham on the cheek.

Graham immediately turned scarlet red.

"Oh, I almost forgot. I brought you something else to speed your recuperation. Something an Irish man on the mend shouldn't be without," Mrs. Reilly said as she handed a flask of Irish whiskey and turned to leave.

"Mrs. Reilly. Will you stay and have a drink with me?" Graham asked nervously.

"I will," Mrs. Reilly said, smiling. "My first name is Rose, by the way."

Byrne was starting to regain consciousness when Mike entered Byrne's hospital room.

"How's the old man, Jacob?" Mike asked.

"I think he'll be okay. He's starting to come to."

"Show him this," Mike said as he handed Jacob a copy of the Philadelphia Inquirer. The headline read, "Retired Admiral Henry Bannister Killed in Boating Accident." The subtitle stated, "Was to Be Philadelphia's New Police Commissioner."

"Father, Dad! Look at this," Jacob said as he placed the paper in front of his father. It took a moment for Byrne to focus. Then he smiled.

"Mike, can you stay with my father for awhile while I go see Molly and wash up a bit?" Jacob asked.

"Sure."

"I'll be back, Dad."

Jacob stopped by the restroom and splashed his face with cold water before he went to the waiting room.

"Oh, Jacob. How's your father?" Molly asked.

"Better, he's awake now."

"That's so wonderful. Here, Mrs. Reilly and I made some sandwiches," Molly said as she handed Jacob a bag.

"Thanks, Molly. I hadn't noticed how hungry I was. Where's Mrs. Reilly?"

"She's visiting with Mr. Graham."

"I should give my respects to George as well. Will you come with me?"

"Yes, of course."

As Molly and Jacob approached Graham's room, they heard laughter. Jacob couldn't remember ever hearing Graham laugh.

"George, I was going to ask how you were, but I can see you're doing well," Jacob said.

"Yeah, I'm okay. How's your father?"

"He just woke up. I think he'll be okay. You know how tough he is. He'll make it," Jacob said. "Molly, Mrs. Reilly, could you give George and me a moment?"

"Of course," Mrs. Reilly said as she ushered Molly out the door. "I'll be back, George."

Jacob waited for the two women to leave, and then he grew serious.

"George, it was the Italians who did this. They were trying to get back at me. I'm sorry," Jacob said.

"You did nothing wrong," Graham said.

"Mike got the guys who shot you and my father. They're dead, and we're going to take care of their bosses soon. I just want you know," Jacob said.

"I'll help."

"No, George. You get better. My father's going to need you more than ever now and so do I," Jacob said. He paused and cocked his head towards the door and back to Graham. "Looks like you a have an admirer, George. I'll send Mrs. Reilly back in."

George blushed.

"Mrs. Reilly, your little Georgie-Porgie is waiting for you," Jacob said, smiling.

"Oh you shush," Mrs. Reilly said as she went back in Graham's room with a smile on her face.

"Molly, I'll have someone drive you home. Jimmy will be home soon and he'll need you. Stay in the house. If you or Jimmy need anything, ask one of the guards."

"What's happening, Jacob?" Molly asked nervously.

"Better you don't know. I just want to keep you and Jimmy safe," Jacob said. Everything will be all right in a week or so.

10

Jacob spent the rest of the day with his father and Graham. At 6 PM he told his father he would be back in the morning, and he and Mike started off to his house to meet with the new crew leaders. Two of Mike's men drove in a separate car in front of them.

The hospital was located at Eighth and Pine Street and the best way to get back to Wishart Street was to take Fifth Street North to Allegheny Avenue and then east on Allegheny to Howard Street and one block South to Wishart.

"Did you speak to Frank?" Jacob asked Mike as they turned onto Fifth Street.

"Yes, everything's ready. The guys are at the house waiting for you."

"Good," Jacob said and paused for a minute. "Mike, look, I want you to know I really appreciate what you have done for Frank and me."

"It's my job, boss," Mike answered.

"No. It's more than a job. You've been a great friend. You're there when we need you. I mean how many times have you pulled my fat out of the fire?" Jacob asked.

"Five or six," Mike said, laughing.

"I mean it, Mike. You're the real deal," Jacob said as he patted Mike's shoulder. "I want you to take charge of all the crews. The leaders will report to you directly and you..." Jacob was interrupted by the crushing impact of a vehicle hitting the back right side of his car.

The impact sprung the driver's side door open and Mike tumbled out onto the street. Two men stepped out of their car, pistols in hand. The driver rounded the cars to the left side and the other man advanced on Jacob. Jacob saw him and pulled his own pistol. As the man appeared in the closed window of the car, Jacob shot him. The window's glass shattered and smashed into the man's face as the bullet hit the man in the throat. He stood there with glass protruding from his face and right eye, holding his neck. His face was red with blood as spurts of his life's fluid came through his fingers. He was choking on his own blood.

Jacob turned to see Mike lying in the street and the second man standing over him with his gun pointed at Mike's head. It seemed to Jacob that everything was happening in slow motion. He pointed the gun at the man and squeezed the trigger. The impact of the bullet spun the man around and he dropped his weapon. Before Jacob could get a second shot off, the man ran south down Fifth Street.

"Mike, Mike! You okay?"

Mike looked up at Jacob and said, "Yeah."

"Holy shit, that was close. Those fucks must have been watching us at the hospital," Jacob said.

"I'm sorry, Jacob. I should have known," Mike said.

"Not your fault, Mike."

Mike got up just as their men in the lead car drove up. They had seen what had happened and immediately turned around. By the time they arrived, it was over.

"Take the plate off," Jacob told the driver as he helped Mike into the car.

The driver took the plate, threw it in the boot, and drove off up Fifth Street. By the time they arrived at Jacob's Wishart Street home, Mike was feeling better.

"How are you, Mike?"

"I'm good. Just sore. Nothing broke. Jacob... thanks."

"Good. Let's go in and talk to the guys."

When Mike and Jacob entered the dining room, Molly was serving Frank, Grady and the ten new crew leaders coffee and cake from the German bakery. He could see the men were enjoying her company and he felt a pang of jealously. He kissed Molly and asked her if she was okay and where Jimmy was. The open affection he showed Molly should have made it clear that this woman was his. "Molly, would you please go to your room and find Jimmy and take him with you? This could get a bit rowdy," Jacob whispered in Molly's ear. Then Jacob greeted each man personally.

When Jacob was finished meeting the new crew leaders, Franklin got up from his normal seat at the table and stood on Jacob's right side. Mike took a place in the back of the room. The men had all stood up as a sign of respect for Jacob's authority.

"Mike, up here, please," Jacob said. Mike took his place on Jacob's left side.

"I want to thank you all for coming. Please sit," Jacob paused for a few seconds and said, "Frank has informed you all that each of you will lead a group of ten men. Consider it like the army. You're the lieutenant in charge. I want you to pick someone you trust to be your second. Grady will still be in charge of the crews from the old Girard Avenue gang. He and all of you will report to Mike," Jacob said as he put his arm around Mike's shoulder.

"I want you and your men to be armed. See Grady or Mike if you need weapons. We're going to war, boys" Jacob said.

The men reacted as he expected. They cheered and laughed, but he could see fear on some of their faces, especially those who had actually been in the war.

"This is not what I wanted, but we can't allow the Italians to continue to kill our people and disrupt our business."

"Fucking wops," one man said.

"Greasy cock suckers," another man yelled.

The others all agreed and let out a litany of slurs and curses. Jacob allowed them a few minutes to vent.

"Okay guys, simmer down," Jacob said and paused for a few seconds as they became quiet again. "Here's what we're going to do. Tonight—and every night until we work this out—you are going to hit their joints. I want them to bleed money. If we can stop their business from operating, they'll be critically wounded. Mike and Grady will have the details.

What I don't want is any unnecessary killing. At some point, we'll have to do business with some of these guys. Other than that, you can do whatever you need to do to shut them down. Any money or goods you get are yours to keep. I want you to share it with your crew and Mike and Grady."

"Fucking affirmative," one man, an ex soldier, said and the others showed their approval with similar comments and curses.

"There's one exception to my no-killing rule. There are two guys I specifically want dead. The first is Franky Capaci. He's the boss of their gang and he's the one who ordered our guys and my father to be killed. The other is Carlo **Pascucci**. He's Capaci's man who planned the killings. Whoever gets them, gets a bonus."

"We'll get 'em boss," one of the men said, and the others voiced their agreement.

"Okay. Let's have some drinks. Mike, break out the Irish, will you? I'll be right back," Jacob said.

Jacob left the room and climbed the stairs to Molly's room. He knocked.

"Come in," Molly said.

"Where's Jimmy?" Jacob asked.

"He's across the street at his friend Gilly's house," Molly answered.

"He knows not to leave the block, doesn't he?"

"Oh yes. Just as you asked."

"Good," Jacob said as he walked over to Molly and kissed her. They embraced for several minutes.

"Jacob, I'm scared," Molly said.

"Me too, Molly, but I have no choice. These animals tried to kill my father. Who's next? You? Jimmy? I have to protect you," Jacob said.

"I know, I know, but please… please be careful."

"There's nothing that can keep me from coming back to you, Molly," Jacob said and kissed her again. "I have to get back. Will you come see me in my room later tonight?"

"I will."

Jacob returned to the men, had a couple shots of Irish whiskey, and sent them, Mike, and Grady off to get ready for the evening raids on the Italians. The house was suddenly very quite. Molly was still in her room. Mrs. Reilly was at the hospital. It was just Jacob and Franklin. Jacob sat looking out the window and Franklin was staring at Jacob.

Jacob noticed Franklin and said, "What the fuck are you looking at?"

"I, Sir, am looking at a fucking leader. A boss. A General."

"Get the fuck outta here," Jacob said.

"No, I mean it, Jacob. These last couple of days you have really taken charge. The men respect you, maybe even fear you," Franklin said.

"And how do you feel about it?" Jacob asked.

"Well I would be very, very jealous if I didn't love you like a little brother," Franklin said as he got up and rubbed Jacob's head.

"You fucking asshole," Jacob said as they both laughed.

At ten o'clock, Mike returned and reported that everything was in motion. He had told the guys to get baseball bats, clubs or chains and to keep their guns in their pockets unless they really needed them.

"Okay. Great job, Mike. Let's go," Jacob said.

"You don't have to go, Jacob. Stay here with Molly. We'll take care of things," Franklin said.

"No fucking way. What kind of boss is that? I'm going!"

"Jesus, Jacob, don't get your panties in a wad. I'm just saying," Franklin said. "Okay, Okay. Let's go."

At midnight, each crew hit their target, breaking down doors and busting up both Italian-run joints and the patrons. Beer and whiskey mixed with blood flowed on the floors. The attacks were so numerous and so intense the Italians could do nothing but try to protect themselves.

It was an intense week. Jacob spent his days at the hospital, his evenings in South Philly busting up the speakeasies, and the early morning hours with Molly who visited him every night after he returned. For five nights, they picked different spots and wreaked havoc. The Italians hit back hard, busting up Jacob's places as well. Neither was making money and they still had not found Capaci or **Pascucci**. Several times the Italians tried to hit the Wishart Street compound, but could not get in.

Despite Jacob's orders, there were several Italian mobsters killed. Two of Jacob's men had also died in the melees. The stress was starting to show on both gangs. With little or no money coming in, the men on both sides were starting to grumble. Amato was waiting patiently for his moment.

Gerardo Amato picked up the phone and dialed.

"Hello?" Jacob answered.

"It's me. Capaci's at 1552 Christian Street, visiting his moulinyan mistress. You know where it is?"

"I'll find it," Jacob answered. "Is **Pascucci** with him?"

"Always," Amato said and hung up.

Jacob called Mike and told him to get his best crew and meet him at his house as soon as he could. He then went over to Franklin's side of the house and told him. Mike showed up with a crew fifteen minutes later.

"Anybody know where 1503 Christian is?" Jacob asked.

"Yeah. It's at Fifteenth and Christian in the negro part of town," one man said.

"Okay, you take Joe and go down there and get the lay of the land. Be very careful. Capaci's there and we are going to take him out tonight," Jacob said.

"You got it, boss," the man said.

"Meet us back at Fifteenth and Market."

"Got it," the man replied as he and Joe left.

The rest of the crew—Franklin, Mike and Jacob drove to Fifteenth and Market. There was a restaurant on the southwest corner of the street and they waited there.

"Did you know that no one can build a building higher than City Hall?" Franklin asked.

"Sure. It's the law," Jacob answered.

"I didn't know that," Mike said.

"Yep, it's the law. It's a beautiful building, isn't it?" Franklin said, looking across the street at the statue of William Penn on the top of the building.

"It's not so pretty when you're inside, waiting for a judge to sentence you," Mike said.

"I guess not. What did you do?" Jacob said.

"You know that grocery store on the corner of Kensington and Front? I stole some fruit when I was ten and got caught," Mike said.

"And?" Franklin asked.

"They let me go. I told the Judge I hadn't eaten in three days and was hungry. It was all bull, but they ate it up," Mike said, laughing.

After about forty-five minutes, the scouts met the crew at the restaurant. They told Jacob that the house was the second one on the east side of the street. The only entrances were the front door and a back door off an alley. There were two guards at both entrances. They didn't know if there were more in the house. They suggested that they could park on Webster Street, the next street west, and Montrose, the next street east.

"What do you think, Frank? Should we take the house or wait until he comes out?" Jacob asked.

"If we wait, we could miss him. We can't get close enough to be sure that we can get him before he gets in his car. Then again, it could be tough to get him in the house. We don't know how many people are inside," Franklin said.

"Mike," Jacob said, "I got an idea. We get some brown or black shoe polish and Frank and me put it on our faces. We pull our collars up and we walk down the street. We look like Negros. They won't pay us any attention until we shoot them," Mike said.

"Could work. We get a few of our guys in the back and they take out the guards when they hear you shoot. Our other guys can be waiting around the corner and when we kill the guards they can come running, break down the door and we see what's inside," Franklin said.

"I agree, but it will be me not Franklin with you, Mike," Jacob said.

"Come on, Jacob. I can do this," Franklin said.

"I know you can do it, but it was my father they tried to kill. You just make sure you get your asses up here as soon as we shoot. Agreed?" Jacob asked.

"You and me, boss," Mike said.

"Agreed," Franklin said.

"Okay then, let's go," Jacob said.

Mike gave the shoeshine boy outside the restaurant a dollar for a can of brown shoe polish and they drove to Fifteenth and Christian. On the way, Mike smeared the shoe polish on Jacob's face and Jacob did the same for Mike. It wasn't perfect but from a distance it would work. They pulled up in front of the church at Sixteenth and Christian and Mike and Jacob got out.

They waited ten minutes until the others got into position and started walking east on Christian. It was a cold night and no one was out.

"You ready, Mike?"

"Yeah. I hope the other guys are ready," Mike said.

"Me too."

As they got closer to the house, one guard elbowed the other and
pointed at the two men walking up the street. "It's just two moulinyans," the
other guard said.

"Hey you two; get on the other side of the fucking street," the first
guard said.

Jacob and Mike kept walking.

"I said, get the fuck on the other side of the street or we'll kick your
asses," the guard said again.

"Sorry, sir, what'd you say?" Jacob said.

"I said, get the fuck..." The guard was interrupted by two bullets rip-
ping through his chest. He fell as the other guard was hit in the head. Jacob
heard the running steps of Frank and the men as he heard several more
shots. "The guys must have gotten the guards in the rear," he said.

When Franklin arrived at the house he motioned Mike and Jacob
away from the door and kicked it in, immediately crouching low. Two bullets whizzed past his head. He shot back and hit a man who was standing at
the stairway to the second floor. In seconds, his men were in the house. They
searched the lower floors and it was empty.

"Capaci must be upstairs," Mike said as he started for the staircase.

"No hold on Mike. Too dangerous," Jacob said. I have an idea. "How
much ammo do we have?"

"Plenty," Mike said.

"Everyone start shooting into the ceiling. Some into the bedroom
above and some in the hallway," Jacob said.

They looked at him as if he were crazy. "Do it!" Jacob yelled.

The men started shooting and Mike and Jacob went up the steps.
When they hit the first floor landing, Carlo **Pascucci** was lying in the hall,
groaning in pain. He had been shot in the groin.

"Is that Pascucci? Mike asked.

"That's him," Jacob said and Mike shot Pascucci in the head twice. "The
fucking prick."

They checked the other rooms and they were empty.

"All clear. Come up," Jacob said. When the men were on the second
floor, he said, "Now do it again."

The men began shooting at the ceiling. Jacob and Mike went up the stairs. No one was in the hallway and the doors were open to the two bedrooms. The bathroom door was closed.

"Mike, check the back bedroom. I'll cover you," Jacob whispered.

Mike checked the room and made a hand signal indicating it was empty. Jacob motioned he would check the front room. When he went into the room, an attractive Negro woman was lying on the bed, whimpering.

"Stay here and shut up and you won't be hurt," Jacob told her. He motioned to Mike that someone had to be in the bathroom.

"Kick it in and stand back," Jacob said.

Mike kicked the door open and moved quickly to the side, expecting to hear gunshots. Nothing happened. Jacob took a quick look into the bathroom. He laughed.

"What the fuck are you laughing at?" Mike asked.

"Take a look. It's okay," Jacob said.

Mike looked through the doorway and starting laughing. Capaci was lying naked in the bathtub. He had run from the front room and jumped in the cast iron tub to avoid the bullets coming through the floor. It was a glorious sight. The boss of the Italian family, naked and huddling in a bathtub. Jacob had literally caught Capaci with his pants down.

"What the fuck do you want?" Capaci screamed. "Do you know who I am?"

"Oh yeah, we know. What's the matter, Capaci; is it cold in here? I thought the boss of the Italians might have a bigger prick," Jacob said, laughing. Mike joined in.

"Get the fuck out of the tub."

"Fuck you, Mick! Shoot me. Get it over with," Capaci screamed.

"Oh no, Capaci. We have other plans for you," Jacob said as he grabbed Capaci by the hair and lifted him from the tub. "Tie his hands, Mike, and get him to the car.

Mike grabbed the tie from the bathroom curtain and tied Capaci's hands behind his back. He pushed Capaci out the door.

"Mike, take him to the Girard Avenue club. Put him in one of the basements. Frank and I will be there soon."

"Give me my fucking robe," Capaci said.

"No. You get nothing, you fucking grease ball," Jacob said.

Franklin had come up the stairs and heard Jacob tell Mike to put Capaci in the car.

"What the fuck are you doing, Jacob? Shoot the cock sucker and let's get out of here."

"No. I have a better idea. Let's go, Frank, before the cops show up. I'll tell you on the way," Jacob replied.

On the way to the Front and Girard, Jacob briefed Franklin. When they were near City Hall, he had the driver stop at a payphone.

"Frank, you got two pennies?" Jacob asked.

"What the fuck! Two cents for a telephone call. Shit, I can buy a pint of milk for that," Franklin complained.

"When's the last time you drank any milk? Give me the pennies," Jacob said.

"Well, just saying. That's a lot for a simple telephone call," Franklin said.

"Okay, okay. You're right. Let me make this call," Jacob said as he dropped the pennies in the slot.

"Hello? This is Amato."

"It's done. Come to the Girard Avenue place to pick up your gift," Jacob said and hung up. "Okay, let's go.

By the time Jacob and Franklin arrived at the Girard Avenue club, Mike had Capaci safe in the basement. Capaci was sitting, still naked, on a wooden chair surrounded by cases of beer.

Franklin bent down and said in Capaci's ear, "Enjoying your visit, you fucking wop bastard?"

Capaci screamed, "Vaffanculo!" and spit on Franklin's shoes.

"What's that you said? You want to suck my dick?"

"It means go fuck yourself up your ass," Capaci yelled. Franklin punched him in his jaw.

"Leave him alone, Frank. Our Friend will want to talk to him," Jacob said.

"Okay," Franklin said and punched Capaci again.

It was another fifteen minutes before Grady came to the basement and announced that Amato had arrived.

"Bring him down," Jacob said.

When Capaci saw Amato, he yelled, "You fucking mother's whore. You cock sucking old fuck! I..." Amato interrupted Capaci by kissing him on the lips. At the same time, he took a knife from his pocket and drew it across Capaci's throat. Capaci's eyes widened in shock as blood squirted from his neck. Amato pushed his head back, widening the gap and making Capaci bleed harder. He then said, "This is how we kill a pig in Sicily." He made the sign of the cross as the blood dripped from his hand.

Amato took a handkerchief from his pocket and wiped the blood from the knife and his hands. He handed the knife to Jacob and said, "A token of our friendship, Jacob. Give me a week or so and we will meet to put our differences aside."

Jacob took the knife and said, "A week then."

"Now if you would be so kind, can you wrap him up? I'll have him to go."

Mike and Grady wrapped Capaci's body in a rug and placed it in Amato's car trunk.

After Amato left, Franklin said, "That is one stone cold wop."

"The guys from the old country are tough. He was giving us a message," Jacob said.

"Oh yeah, and what's that?"

"It's better to be my friend than my enemy," Jacob said.

11

"Jacob, I am with child," Molly said.

It had been almost ten years since the war with the Italians. Amato kept his promise and Jacob's North Philadelphia Gang and the Italian's South Philadelphia Gang remained at peace and worked together for their mutual benefit. The alliance solidified both Jacob's and Amato's power and the soldiers in both gangs were content with their pieces of the pie. Amato had some early resistance to his leadership but his fast and ruthless actions put an end to it and firmed up his reputation of being the most feared and loved gangster in South Philadelphia.

Amato had a firm but fair hand with his soldiers. He made sure they had enough money to care for their families, and in cases where they needed assistance, he was most generous. But those who broke his old country rules were swiftly dealt with.

Amato was also community minded. He knew that if the people were behind you they would keep the authorities away from you. He was a frequent contributor to local charities and churches. In addition, he provided funds to enlarge the Ninth Street market, ensuring that his Italian neighbors could always find the foods they loved.

Jacob was able to build his illegal organization to encompass all of North Philadelphia. He married Molly Sims in 1924 and adopted Jimmy as his own. Jimmy was now nineteen years old and in his second year of college at the University of Pennsylvania. Jacob's wasn't the only marriage during this time. Mrs. Reilly had helped nurse George Graham and Charles Byrne to health after the Capaci shootings. She became very close to Graham and at first, she and George became lovers. In 1925, they were married.

Charles Byrne recuperated but was paralyzed from his waist down. He maintained control over his construction business, but as he grew older, Jacob had to become more involved in the business. The elder Byrne lost a lot of money during the various stock market crashes of 1929 and 1930. His construction business suffered as no one could buy houses or build factories.

It was a different story for Jacob's other less legal business interest. It seemed the less work a man had to do the more they drank. His illegal speakeasies, prostitution and gambling operations were doing very well.

Franklin, with the help of Mike and Grady, kept the organization running, while Jacob put his abilities to creating strategies to keep them strong. The Twenty-First Amendment to the US Constitution was about to make manufacturing and selling alcoholic beverages legal again and it was changing everything.

"Did you say something, Molly?" Jacob asked as he folded and placed the newspaper on the table.

"I said, I am with child. I'm pregnant."

"Pregnant!" Jacob said, looking at Molly dumbfounded.

"Yes!"

"That's tremendous! When? How?" Jacob asked.

"Well, I think you know how. Four weeks, I think," Molly said.

Jacob rose from the table and kissed Molly on the lips and said. "I'm very happy."

"Oh. That's a relief. I wasn't sure you would be."

"Why wouldn't I be? I love kids, especially our kids," Jacob said.

Jacob and Molly had three other children, not counting Jimmy. Mercy, who was named after Jacob's mother, was going on nine. Charles, or as they called him Charlie, was seven and Jacob Jr. was five.

"We have to tell Rose," Jacob said. He had taken to calling Mrs. Reilly by her first name after she married George Graham. He just could not get his head around calling her Mrs. Graham.

"Oh, she knows," Molly said.

"You told her before me?"

"Well she's like my Ma, you know," Molly said.

"Who else knows?"

"I think George. After all, they are married and most married people talk to each other about such things," Molly said.

Molly's own mother had died when Molly was seven years old and her father raised her. He was a drunk and abused her so when her first husband James asked her to run away and marry him she readily agreed. Molly was just 15 years old at the time.

Franklin knocked on the doorframe and asked, "You two busy?"

"No; come in Frank," Molly said.

"Congratulations," Frank said and kissed Molly on the cheek and took Jacob's hand and shook it.

Jacob looked at Molly and she said, "I swear I never told him!"

"Told me what? Oh, no; Rose just told me yesterday. I swear," Franklin said and held his right hand up. "Got any names picked out? If it's a boy, Franklin is a good name," Franklin said, laughing.

"Am I the only one who didn't know?" Jacob asked, shaking his head.

"Well, I'll leave you two to your business," Molly said and quickly left the room.

"Why so touchy, Jacob?" Franklin asked.

"I'm not. You know that Molly and the kids get away with murder with me. I just had to act surprised and a little hurt. Keeps her on her toes. My dad told me a couple days ago. George told him," Jacob said.

"Are there no secrets in this Family?" Franklin asked, laughing.

"Only the ones that count. Speaking of that, how are the licenses going?" Jacob asked.

Jacob and Franklin had secretly been preparing for the appeal of prohibition that was due on December 5th, by working with some bureaucrats in the state and city governments. The bureaucrats were creating the proper documentation to get licenses to serve alcohol for most of Jacob and Franklin's speakeasies and two breweries. Some would become restaurants. Some would remain clubs or bars and several would remain illegal because they had a brisk gambling business.

"My guys in the capital say they expect the new amendment to take effect on December 5th and we can open, with licenses, the next day," Franklin said.

"That's great, Frank. Finally, we'll be almost all legal. I just wish the state had allowed private companies to own liquor stores," Jacob said.

"Yeah, well, the politicians are more corrupt than we are. They know there's a lot of money to be made. I bet most of them have a hand in supplying the new State Stores," Franklin said.

"I am sure of that," Jacob said.

"How's the construction business going? Sorry I haven't had time to help out."

"Not good. There are no building projects right now, just repair work. We had to lay off most of the employees. I feel sick about it, but there was no choice."

"It's not your fault. It was those fucking greedy bankers and politicians that fucked things up," Franklin said.

"My dad's not doing well. He mopes around all the time reliving the old days. The only joy he has is when the kids visit him. Funny, considering how bad a father he was, he's a great grandfather. Gives those kids every-thing," Jacob said.

"That's what grandpop's are for," Franklin said.

"And what about uncles? You're the worst. Go get your own kids to spoil," Jacob said.

"Ha. I am not the fathering type. That would cut down on my philan-dering. Anyway, I can spoil your kids and send them back over here. Can't do that if I had my own," Franklin said.

"The perpetual bachelor. There is no changing you."

"I guess not."

What about the other things we've been talking about?" Jacob asked.

Jacob and Franklin had been discussing other lines of work they could do when booze became legal. There were several being considered, to add to their prostitution and gambling work.

"Like I said before, I think the numbers racket is great for us. We already have gambling. I have two guys working it and then we have been recruit-ing the existing numbers organizations," Franklin said.

"Okay let's do that. I agree that its perfect. Any of these other numbers people giving you a problem?" Jacob asked.

"A little, but we are able to convince them. Most are mom and pop operations. Milkmen, candy store owners, some homemakers. There are a couple larger crews, but I think we can persuade them."

"Good, what about second story?"

"Grady wants to take that on. He has some experience and he'll orga-nize small groups from the crews. We have fences lined up," Franklin said.

"Remember, no capers in Kensington or the rest of the poorer areas of North Philly. And nothing in the Italian area in South Philly," Jacob said.

"Right. He'll stick to the main line, our part of Jersey and some towns outside Philly. Elkins Park and Jenkintown might be good," Franklin agreed.

"Anything else?" Jacob asked.

"Protection and drugs," Franklin said.

"I don't like the protection racket. Just doesn't seem right to take from our own people. I know Amato does it and they make a fortune. I don't want that," Jacob said

"I agree. It's not for us. Some of the Italians are getting into drugs. Heroin, for example," Franklin said.

"Let's hold off on that and we'll see where it goes," Jacob said.

"Good money in drugs, Jacob."

"I know, but I want to see how it shakes out."

"So I guess that's it?" Franklin asked.

"We are now in the numbers and second story business. If that's all, I need to go see my father. Want to come? Rose and Graham will be there," Jacob said.

"No, I'll drop by another day. I'm meeting with Amato to work out the numbers deal. They have a few bookies located north of Market Street," Franklin said.

"Let him keep them. See if you can get 20% off the top," Jacob said.

"I was thinking 25%," Franklin said.

"You going to be in the office later today?" Jacob asked.

Jacob and Frank had converted nine homes several years ago on their side of Wishart Street and turned them into offices. The old candy store was now offices for their accountants. Since the peace with the Italians, security wasn't an important matter so they moved their crew members, who once lived in the homes, to ones on Allegheny Avenue. As the organization grew, they needed office space. It made sense to make it as close as possible.

"I'll be there," Franklin said.

Jacob drove to his father's house, on Broad Street, in his new 1933 Duesenberg Roadster. He loved the car and drove it whenever he could, which wasn't often because the car wasn't suitable for the children. They would have to ride in the rumble seat, not a great place for three rambunctious kids. When he had to travel with his children, he took the Cadillac Fleetwood. On rare occasions, he and Molly would drive to the country in the Duesenberg alone. Those drives in the country were always a prelude to a great night of sex.

His father's home hadn't changed in the last ten years, but the surrounding buildings had. Several large mansions had been rehabilitated prior to the Depression, but were now empty and for sale at very attractive prices. One of the mansions was next to his father's home and Jacob had contemplated buying it when it went on the market. He hadn't acted because of the uncertainly of the economy, and with the IRS and Capone's indictment for tax evasion. Now with Prohibition being repealed and his plan to open legitimate clubs and legitimate cash flow increasing, it might be a good investment. He made a mental note to check on it.

Jacob knocked on his father's door. Ever since the attempt on his life and the event that put him in a wheelchair, the elder Byrne had made sure all his doors were locked at all times. Rose, now Mrs. Graham, answered the door.

"Jacob! Oh, it's so good to see you. Come in," Rose said as she hugged and kissed Jacob on the cheek.

"Rose, you act as if you never see me. I was just here on Sunday," Jacob said.

"I know, but I miss seeing you and Franklin every day. Where is that big lug?" Rose asked.

"He's working. Said he would come by Sunday for dinner."

"How's Molly and my dear children?" Rose asked.

"Molly is great. She sends her love. She had a meeting with one of her charities and couldn't come with me. The kids are fine. They miss their Nanny Rose," Jacob said.

"Aww, how sweet. But I think they love the candy I get for them from Emily's more," Rose said, laughing.

"Rose, how's my father doing?" Jacob asked.

"He's pretty much the same. Up one day, down another. He seems a bit tired," Rose said.

"Is he ill?"

"He wants to speak to you about something. That's why he asked you over," Rose replied.

"What?"

"He'll have to tell you himself, Jacob," Rose said.

"Oh, very mysterious," Jacob said mockingly.

"He's in his office. Go ahead. He's been waiting for you. Can I get you anything? Coffee? A drink?"

"No thank you. I'll see you before I leave."

Jacob looked at the office door for a minute. He found it odd that he had grown closer to his father as an adult than he could ever have as a child. Nearly being murdered had changed something in the old man. He became more caring as he aged. It could be because he was confined to a wheelchair and needed people more or it was simply due to the fact that near death makes you think more about how you live your life.

It certainly wasn't because he wanted to make amends so he could enter the pearly gates when he left this world. The old man didn't believe in god or any religion. A few years back he had told Jacob, half in jest, "When I die, just shove a bone up my ass and toss me in the alley. The dogs will take care of the rest."

Jacob took a deep breath and opened the door to the office. His father was sitting behind his cherry wood desk reading the newspaper.

"How you doing, Dad?" Jacob asked as he leaned over the desk and shook his father's hand.

"As good as can be expected for a guy who can't walk, can't fuck and has to be wheeled around in chair," Byrne replied.

"From what I hear—I won't say from who—you have lady friends in for visits several times a week. It doesn't seem as though you're having too much trouble in that department," Jacob said.

"Okay, so I can fuck! But it's not the same. Now I have to buy it. When I was younger I never had to pay," Byrne complained.

"Other than that, how are you feeling?" Jacob asked.

"Look at this!' Byrne said as he turned the newspaper around so Jacob could see.

"What?" Jacob asked, puzzled.

"There, the article about the two fucking idiots who crashed their airplane in the Schuylkill River," Byrne said. "These airplanes are too dangerous. Man wasn't meant to fly."

"It's the future. Anyway, stop avoiding my question. How are you feeling?" Jacob asked.

"Sit down, Jacob. You want a drink or something?" Byrne asked.

"No thank you. Rose already asked me," Jacob replied.

Byrne looked at his son for a moment and slumped his shoulders. "I have cancer… The doc says I'll be dead in six months."

"What?" Jacob asked in a daze. His mind could not get around the idea of what his father had just said. The shock stunned him and he sat in silence for a minute before he asked, "Did you see other doctors? There has to be something they can do."

"I've seen three of those fucking quacks and they all say the same thing. I have cancer. One says I'll be gone in three months, another says a year. They don't know any fucking thing," Byrne said.

"But…" Jacob was interrupted by his father.

"No Jacob. I have a death sentence and I have to prepare for it," Byrne said. "I've left you everything I have."

"I don't…" Jacob was interrupted again.

"Just let me talk," Byrne said. "I am leaving you everything. The house, the company, and what money I have. I want you to put whatever you can away for the kids. Maybe they can go to college or something. Be sure Jimmy gets a share. He's a good kid. I'm also leaving some money for Graham and Rose. It would also make me happy if you keep them on the payroll when I am gone."

"Of course! They're family, but you're talking like you've given up. There has to be something we can do. We'll get the best doctors and..." Byrne interrupted Jacob again.

"No. I've done that. All of the docs agree on one thing. I will die and it won't be pleasant. I don't want the kids to see me like that," Byrne said. A tear trickled down his cheek.

Jacob's mind was still reeling, but the reality was slowly seeping in. "What can I do for you, Dad? Anything you want, just let me know."

"You could send Mike over and have him put two in the back of my head," Byrne said, laughing.

"What? You th..." Byrne interrupted Jacob.

"Just kidding, son. Trying to lighten up the mood here. I don't want to spend the rest of my life, whatever I have left, wallowing in self pity. Fuck that!" Byrne said.

"I guess I understand that," Jacob said.

"There is something you can do, though."

"Name it and it's done," Jacob said.

"Good. Then bring Molly and the kids over for dinner tomorrow night. We'll have a real family get together with Graham and Rose."

"Done. Anything else?" Jacob asked.

"No," Byrne said and paused for a few seconds. "Just… please don't tell the kids about my cancer."

The next day Jacob gathered the three kids and Molly, packed them in the Cadillac and drove to his father's house for dinner.

"Are we here yet, Dad?" Charlie asked. Seven-year-old Charlie Byrne was the spitting image of his father. His hair was black and his eyes a beautiful green. Charlie was a good student and often praised by his teachers. Jacob Junior, or Jakey as they called him, was younger than Charlie and he idolized his brother. That, of course, didn't stop them from fighting and Jakey more often than not got the best of Charlie. Jakey looked more like Molly with his blond hair and light complexion.

"It's 'Are we there yet,' not 'here yet,' stupid," Mercy said. Older than both her brothers, Mercy saw herself as her brothers' protector and teacher. Mercy had auburn hair, a throwback from one of her mother's grandparents, and her father's beautiful green eyes. She had a sweet disposition, but if anyone threatened or even talked bad about the family, she, without hesitation or fear, attacked them verbally or physically. Once a twelve-year-old boy from Lippincott Street was pushing Charlie around and Molly gave the boy a bloody nose. From that moment on, children who knew the Byrne kids played nice.

"You're stupid," Charlie replied.

"You're both stupid," Jakey said, laughing.

"Okay, okay! Keep it down. None of you is stupid. Five more minutes. We'll be there," Jacob said.

"How long is five minutes?" Jakey asked.

Simultaneously Mercy and Charlie said, "Oh shut up, Jakey." And this started another verbal battle between the Byrne children.

"Stop it. Sit there and be quite for a while," Molly said sternly.

As they traveled north on Leigh Avenue, Mercy sat quietly, perturbed that her mother had reproached her, looking out the car window. She was interested to see a long line of people outside the Catholic mission.

"Ma, what are those people doing over there?" Mercy asked as she pointed to the Mission building.

"They're getting free food," Molly replied.

"Why?"

"Well, these last years have been very difficult and many people have lost their jobs…some even their houses. They have no money to buy food, so some charities help out," Molly explained.

"We have money, don't we?" Mercy asked.

"Yes we do."

"So why don't we give those people some money so they can buy houses and food?" Molly asked.

"We do give money to the charities, Mercy, to help buy food and clothes. But we can't give enough to help everyone," Molly said.

"I feel bad for them," Mercy said.

"I'll tell you what. Tomorrow you and I will go to the mission and volunteer to help serve people food. First, we'll stop at the American store and buy some food to donate. Would you like that?"

"Yes, yes," Mercy said excitedly. "Can I pick out the food?"

Dinner was pleasant. Old Man Byrne was very attentive to the children, making sure they were well fed and that he had their favorite desserts. When dinner was finished, they all retired to the sitting room.

"Mercy, I have something for you," Byrne said.

"What is it, Grandpop?" Mercy asked excitedly.

"I want you to have your grandmother's jewelry," Byrne said as he handed Mercy a heavy jewelry case. "You know your grandmother's name was also Mercy?"

"I know, Grandpop," Mercy said as she took the box and almost dropped it. "Ohhh! This is heavy."

"Open it," Byrne said.

Mercy did as he asked and looked in awe. There were several large diamond rings, necklaces, bracelets and a beautiful jeweled broche. Byrne picked out a diamond-encrusted locket on a gold chain.

"Here, I want you to wear this, Mercy," Byrne said as he fixed the gold and diamond-encrusted locket around Mercy's neck. "Inside is a picture of your grandmother and one of me. I want you to have something to remember both of us by.

"I will, Grandpop. I'll never take it off. Thank you so much!" Mercy said.

Byrne patted her on the head, kissed her cheek, and said, "Sweet Mercy. Charlie, I have something for you as well. I've told you that my father was a Calvary Officer in the Pennsylvania Regulars during the Civil War. I want you to have his sword, coat and hat. Be proud of what he did for this country."

"I will, Grandpop. Thank you," Charlie said.

"And Jakey, I have something for you as well," Byrne said.

"What is it?" Jakey asked in excitement.

"First, I want you to promise me that you won't play with my gift until you're older. Will you promise?" Byrne asked.

"Yes, Grandpop," Jakey replied, crossing his fingers behind his back.

"Okay then, here. This was your great grandfather's Henry repeating rifle, and his Colt .44. Take a look at them and we'll let your dad put them in a safe place for you," Byrne said.

"Grandpop, I love these! Thank you," Jakey said as he ran to Byrne and kissed his cheek.

"Molly, I selected a very special piece from my wife's jewelry for you," Byrne said as he handed her a necklace made of white and black pearls. Attached to it was a diamond-rimmed black opal crucifix. "My wife Mercy was a very religious woman and she loved this very much."

"Father, this is so beautiful. Are you sure you don't want to keep it?" Molly asked in humility.

"I can think of no other person I would want to have it more than you, Molly," Byrne said.

"Thank you Father. I just don't know what to say," Molly said as she kissed Byrne on the forehead.

"Jacob, here's some paperwork I want you to put in your safe for me. You'll know when to open it," Byrne said, looking Jacob in the eyes.

"Okay, Dad."

"Tell Jimmy I think he is a fine kid and to keep up his studies. Give him this envelope when the time comes," Byrne said and gave Jacob another envelope.

"I will, Dad."

"Well, if you don't mind, I am getting tired and need to get some rest. I love you all," Byrne said. He hugged and kissed the children and Molly, and then Jacob stuck out his hand. Instead, Byrne hugged Jacob for the first time in his life.

"Take care of the family, Jacob. Family is important," Byrne said in Jacob's ear. "I only wish I knew that when I was younger."

"I will, Dad," Jacob said, thinking how out of character this was for his father. He had a pang of fear, but he didn't know why.

When the family was gone, Byrne asked Rose to get him a double shot of whiskey and had Graham roll him into his office. Rose brought the drink to the office and placed it in front of him.

"Thanks, Rose. You know I never tell you this enough, but both of you have made it a lot easier for me after I was shot. I appreciate that. Now go to bed. Tomorrow will be a big day," Byrne said.

As Rose closed the office door, she asked Graham, "What's going on tomorrow? I didn't know we had anything special planned."

"Don't know," Graham replied and closed the door.

Byrne picked up his cat Shamus and said, "Well old boy, we've been together for a long time. Don't you worry; Rose will take good care for you." He put the cat down, picked up a picture of his wife Mercy, and kissed it. He placed it on the desk, picked up the glass and drank the whiskey in one gulp. Then he opened the desk drawer, pulled out a Colt automatic, placed the barrel against his heart, and pulled the trigger.

12

Charles Byrne's funeral was one of the largest ever held in North Philadelphia. Politicians, local business owners and appreciative homeowners vied to show their respect. The service was held at Mulligan's Funeral Home located at Front Street near Tiago Avenue and Byrne was buried in the Arlington Cemetery, where all religious denominations were accepted. As a suicide, Byrne could not be buried in The Holy Sepulcher, the Catholic cemetery where his wife Mercy was interned.

Because of his new responsibilities, Jacob moved Molly and the children to his father's home and relocated the Wishart Street offices to a mansion a few homes away from his. He suggested that Franklin buy the mansion that was for sale next to his father's home. Franklin agreed.

It had been five months since Jacob had buried his father. He often found himself reflecting on the tumultuous relationship they had shared together. However, these were short-lived reflections as the responsibilities of the construction business, his transition of the illegal activities and the administration of his father's estate had kept him very busy.

As busy as Jacob was he had promised himself that he would always spend Sundays with his family. Since his father's death, these Sundays included a trip to Arlington Cemetery or The Holy Sepulcher to pay respects to his parents. While Molly was at Mass, Jacob would pack the kids into the Cadillac and always take them there first thing in the morning.

"Mercy, Charlie, Jakey—you ready for our trip?" Jacob yelled over the din of noise created by his playing children.

"Oh Jacob, I forgot to tell you. I have a fundraiser at Church today and wanted the children to come with me," Molly said.

"No. I have to go see Grandpop," Mercy said.

"Not today, Mercy. You need to come with me."

"No mom," Mercy retorted.

"Molly, you take Charlie and Jakey. Let Mercy come with me. I need her to help with the flowers," Jacob said as he winked at Molly.

"Okay," Molly replied.

"Oh thank you ma!" Mercy said as she hugged her mother.

"We'll be back by lunch. Will you be done by then?" Jacob asked Molly.

"We should be. Maybe we can have lunch at Bookbinders. Do you think you can get us in?" Molly asked.

"No problem. We'll see you around twelve," Jacob said. "You ready Mercy?"

"Yes Papa."

"We'll take the Duesy today. How about that?" Jacob asked.

"Yeah! I love that car," Mercy said. "Can we drive by the old neighborhood?"

"I guess so. Do you miss the old house, Mercy?" Jacob asked.

"Sometimes I do, but I love Grandpop's house, too."

Jacob lifted Mercy over the car door and put her into the seat next to his. As he did so, he reflected on how Mercy, at just nine years old, seemed so much older. While most kids her age were understandably most interested in playing, Mercy wanted to take care of people who were disadvantaged. She actually suggested that for her birthday, which was next month, Jacob and Molly give money to the Children's Hospital instead of buying her gifts. Mercy, he thought, was a kid with an old soul. He kissed her on the head and said, "You ready?"

"Yes Papa, let's go," Mercy said.

Jacob turned north on Broad Street and then took Allegheny east to Howard Street. When he turned east on Wishart, Mercy became very excited.

"I love this street, Papa!" Mercy said.

"Me too, Mercy. Me too," Jacob said.

"Papa, where are all the people?"

"No one lives here now. We moved; Uncle Frank moved. We moved the offices too. Many of the people who worked for me have moved as well," Jacob said.

"That's sad, Papa."

"When things get better I'll have our side of the street turned into single homes again and then people will move in," Jacob explained.

"When will things get better?"

"No one knows, Mercy. I hope soon. Too many people don't have jobs and so many have lost their homes. We'll just wait and see."

Mercy started to grin.

"What are you smiling about?" Jacob asked as he rubbed Mercy's head.

"I was thinking that since we aren't using the old house, can we let those people who lost their houses live there?" Mercy asked.

"Oh you were, were you? I don't know, Mercy. It not so easy," Jacob explained, not quite sure how to handle this one.

"Oh please, please, pretty please," Mercy said.

"I'll think about it. But now it's time to see Grandpop," Jacob said to placate Mercy.

Arlington Cemetery was near Drexel Hill, which was southwest of North Philly. During the forty-five-minute drive, Mercy continued talking about using the abandoned houses for poor people. She even had a plan to go to the vacant land north of the city, where many people had erected shacks made of old wood or tin. She would find families with children and invite them to live on Wishart Street until they could find work and get their own home.

Jacob was thankful when they arrived at Arlington, when Mercy's attention was now on her grandfather. He couldn't help but feel very proud of a girl who thought so much of others and was so driven to achieve her own ideas. He shook his head as if to clear his mind when he wondered what she would be like when she was an adult.

Jacob drove to the new area of the cemetery and parked the Due-senberg. He and Mercy walked twenty yards to Charles Byrne's mausoleum. Mercy reached up and placed the flowers in the holder next to the door. She bowed her head and said a prayer she had memorized. Jacob watched her and whispered a greeting to his father. Out of the corner of his eye, he noticed a car pull up across the field. Another unfortunate family visiting a departed love one, he thought.

When Mercy was finished with her prayer, he sat her on the marble bench in front of the door and, as was their custom, started to tell a story about his father. As he began the story, he noticed two men getting out of the car that had driven up across the field. They were well-dressed and wearing fedoras. A father and son who, perhaps, had lost his mother. He felt a pang of sorrow when this reminded him of his own mother. Some-thing made him look up again and when he did, the two men were running towards Mercy and himself.

He grabbed Mercy and yelled. "Come on Mercy, we have to leave."

"But we just got here. I don't want..." Mercy said, but was interrupted when Jacob picked her up and started running to the Duesenberg. "What's wrong, Papa?"

Jacob placed her on the seat and said, "Get down, Mercy. On the floor."

"But wha—" Again Mercy was interrupted, this time by the rattle of an automatic rifle. The bullets hit the rumble seat as Jacob dove for the driver's seat. Mercy jumped to the floor. Bullets hit the spare tire on the back of the car as Jacob sped off. He could see in his rearview mirror that the two men were running back to their car. They're not done yet, he thought.

"Mercy, stay down. Don't get up no matter what happens," Jacob yelled as he turned onto State Road and towards Philadelphia. The men weren't far behind. He heard the automatic reverberate as the bullets hit the car again. He pushed the gas pedal to the floor. The Duesy responded with a lurch forward. He gained some space between his car and his pursuers. Reaching down under his seat, he grabbed his Colt .45 automatic. Jacob saw a bend in the road ahead and once he negotiated the turn he quickly pulled the car to the side of the road and got out. He didn't have long to wait when the Lincoln chasing them appeared around the curve. He held his pistol with two hands to steady it and fired three rounds at the driver.

The Lincoln veered off the road and into a clump of trees. Jacob jumped back in the Duesy and drove off as fast as he could. Once he saw that no one was chasing them any longer he told Mercy she could sit up again. There was no answer.

In a panic he said it again. "Mercy, you can get up."

"Papa, I'm bleeding," Mercy whimpered.

Jacob slammed on the brakes and pulled over at the corner of Market and Forty-Eighth Street. He pulled Mercy up to the seat. "Where does it hurt, Mercy?" Jacob asked in a panic.

"It doesn't hurt, Papa," Mercy said in a weak voice.

He saw then that a bullet had hit her in the arm and that she was bleeding profusely. A man sitting on the corner saw them and asked if there was anything he could do.

"Where's the nearest hospital?" Jacob asked.

"Pennsy, I guess," the man answered.

"Can you drive?"

"What?"

"I said can you fucking drive?"

"Yeah, bu—" Jacob interrupted the man and said, "Get the fuck in and drive us to the hospital. Make it fast."

The man did as Jacob asked and Jacob sat in the passenger seat with Mercy on his lap, pressing on the wound to stop the blood.

"I need help here! Get me a doctor. My little girl has been hurt," Jacob yelled as he entered the hospital.

Several nurses ran to Jacob and took Mercy from his arms, rushing her to a room. A doctor followed them in. Jacob ran up to the door but was stopped by the doctor. "Tell me what happened," the doctor asked.

"She was shot. In the arm," Jacob answered

"Okay, please stay here. It is better if we can work on her without others in the room.

"But...."

The doctor interrupted Jacob and said, "Really, it's better for your girl. Please." The doctor turned and shut the door behind him without waiting for a response.

Jacob stood staring at the door for a few minutes and then remembered the man who had driven him to the hospital.

"Here! Here's some cab money. I really appreciate your driving us here," Jacob said as he handed the man two one-hundred dollar bills. "What's your name?"

"Nate. Thank you, mister. I hope your little girl is okay."

"Me too, Nate. Here, take my card. In a couple of weeks come visit me," Jacob said.

Jacob called Franklin and explained what had happened. He warned him to get the men together and asked him to find Molly and the kids and bring them to the hospital.

An hour passed before Molly and the kids arrived. Molly was hysterical and had to be sedated. Charlie and Jakey were crying. Thankfully, Rose and George Graham arrived shortly after Molly and she took the two boys to the cafeteria to get ice cream.

Another thirty minutes passed before the doctor opened the door and walked up to Jacob. "Mr. Byrne, Mercy's okay. She lost a lot of blood, but we stopped the bleeding. The bullet passed through her left arm. It is a miracle it didn't hit the bone. I'm afraid however; she may have trouble using her arm in the future."

The wave of relief that came over Jacob was unlike anything he had ever felt before. He felt happy, sad, tired and especially rage, at the people who had hurt his little girl.

"Can we see her, Doc?" Jacob asked.

"In a while. We had to give her something and she is still very groggy. I'll let you know," the doctor replied.

Jacob slumped back into the waiting room chair, suddenly and totally deflated. He closed his eyes and said a prayer of thanks to a god he did not believe in.

"Jacob, who did this?" George Graham asked in a tone that even frightened Jacob.

"I don't know yet, but I'll find out," Jacob answered.

"And when you do, you won't be keeping me away like you did with Capaci. That little girl is like my own grandchild," Graham said as he turned suddenly so Jacob would not see him wipe the tear from his eye.

"I wouldn't think of it, George."

"How is she?" Graham asked tentatively.

"The doc says she'll be alright. We can see her soon."

Graham sat down heavily in the chair next to Jacob suddenly and said, "That's good Jacob. That's good."

"Can you find Rose and the kids and tell them the good news?" Jacob said.

"What about Molly?" George asked.

"She's still out. Doc gave her something. I'll tell her as soon as she wakes up."

When Franklin was finished setting up security and giving Mike and Grady some last minute orders, he came to the waiting room.

"Any word yet, Jacob?"

"She's okay. They stopped the bleeding and the doc says she'll be okay," Jacob said.

"Oh, thank fucking God," Franklin said as he took the chair next to Jacob. He put his hands to his eyes and rubbed them for a minute. "Did you see anything? Could you recognize them?" Franklin asked.

"No. Not really. Everything went so fast. I know I hit the driver. See if one of our friends in blue can find out who he is. I think we were at the intersection of State Road and West Chester Pike when I shot him."

"Okay, I'll call Murphy. He has some clout," Franklin said.

"Thanks, Frank."

"Don't worry, Jacob. Whoever did this will wish they were never born," Franklin said as he left the waiting room.

"And Frank! Make it snappy," Jacob called after him. "You and I have some work to do." Jacob then walked over to the room in which the doctors had put Molly.

13

"You son-of-a-bitch grease ball bastard! Who hired you?" Jacob yelled as he drove his fist into the man's groin.

The man screamed and said, "I don't know. I swear. Just kill me and get it over with."

"It won't be that easy for you. You shot my daughter, you fucking cunt," Jacob yelled while stabbing an ice pick in the man's knee. The man screamed again.

"You have something to tell us? Or should I work on the other knee?" Jacob asked as he lowered the tip of the ice pick onto the man's kneecap.

"No. Don't! It was Angelo Adone," the man said, tears filling his eyes.

"Who's he with?"

"No… I can't. My family. He'll kill them," the man said.

Jacob drove the ice pick into the man's other knee. The man screamed and said, "Okay, okay. Please stop. He's with the Chicago outfit."

"Why are they after me?" Jacob asked, surprised.

"I swear I don't know," the man said, sobbing.

"Where's this Adone character?"

"I don't know. I don't know. I swear on my kid's lives."

Jacob moved to the back of the chair the man was tied to and whispered in the man's ear. "I swear that Adone will never hurt your family." Then he drove the ice pick through the back of the man's neck and upward into his brain.

"Grady, take care of this, will you?" Jacob asked, pointing to the corpse of the man he had just killed. "What about the other shooter, Mike? Where's he?"

"Murphy told us he's at Hahnemann. Looks like you got him in the neck and the shoulder. Frank's over there seeing if he can get to him," Mike answered.

"Did Murphy have any other information?"

"Just that both men are Italian and from Detroit. Do you think Amato is involved with this?" Mike asked.

"I don't know. It just doesn't make sense to me. We're both making lots of cash. Why would he do this and fuck up our perfect operation?" Jacob said.

"Who knows why the wops do what they do," Mike said.

"Let's get the full picture before we act. We need to find Angelo Adone. Get some feelers out and see what you come up with."

"You got it," Mike said. "Maybe Frank will get something."

Franklin entered the doctor's lounge on the second floor of the hospital. He grabbed a white coat and a surgical mask. He put the mask in the coat pocket and put the coat on. He then took the stairs to the main lobby where he approached the nurse's station.

"Italian fellow brought in yesterday. Shot in the neck. I need a room number," Franklin said with authority.

"That's Mr. Baglio, doctor. He's in room 325," the nurse answered.

"Thanks."

Franklin took the stairs to the third floor. There was a cop stationed outside Baglio's room, so Franklin took out the surgical mask, placed it over his nose and mouth, and approached the man.

"Have you been in this room? Had any contact with Baglio?" Frank asked in an urgent voice.

"Yes... Why?" the police officer asked with concern.

"This man has smallpox. You need to get an inoculation immediately," Franklin said.

"I had that when I was a teenager," the cop answered.

"You need it again. It only lasts a couple of years," Franklin lied.

"What do I do?"

"Go down to room 101 and ask for Dr. McCray. Tell him Dr. Smith sent you and you have been exposed to Smallpox. He'll take care of you," Franklin said.

"I can't leave my post."

"You must get that inoculation. Do you know what smallpox can do to you? To your family? I'll wait here until you get back. Now hurry," Franklin implored.

"Okay. Don't let anyone in," the cop ordered as he rushed off.

"Okay."

When the officer left, Franklin entered the room and locked the door. Baglio was awake.

"You a doctor?" Baglio asked. Franklin didn't answer. "Can you tell that fat bitch nurse to get me some real food? This is garbage," Baglio said as he pushed the food tray off the table.

"Sure, Mr. Baglio. But let me take a look at the wound on your neck first," Franklin said as he removed the bandage.

"Is it okay?" Baglio asked.

"You were lucky, Mr. Baglio. The bullet just missed your external carotid artery. Just a nick and you would be dead in seconds," Franklin said.

"Yeah!"

"You see, it's right here," Franklin lightly touched the bullet's entry wound, to which Baglio flinched. "And the bullet went in, like this," Franklin said as he dug his finger deep into the wound.

Baglio screamed in pain. "What the fuck are you doing!"

Franklin pulled a knife from his pocket, replaced his finger with the point of the knife, and put his other hand over Baglio's mouth. "Quiet, now. You don't want to make me nervous. Feel that? That's my knife very near that artery I mentioned. Understand? Blink your eyes if you do."

Baglio closed and opened his eyes.

"Okay, good. Now I have a few questions for you. If I don't get a good answer I'll cut that artery. Understand? Franklin asked in a low and calm voice.

Baglio closed and opened his eyes.

"Who sent you to kill Jacob Byrne? I am taking my hand from your mouth. If you yell, you die. Okay?"

Baglio closed and opened his eyes.

Franklin took his hand away from Baglio's mouth. "Adone."

"Adone. Is that his first name?" Franklin asked.

"Angelo Adone."

"And who does this Adone work for?"

"Chicago mob," Baglio said.

"You don't say. Why would they want Byrne dead?"

"He didn't tell me nothing, except to kill Byrne and Garrett."

"Where is Adone now?" Franklin asked.

"He's here in Philly."

"Where?"

"All I know is we met him in the lobby of the Bellevue," Baglio said.

There was a bang on the door. "Hey! Open up in there. What are you doing?" A voice behind the door asked.

"I want you to give Adone a message for me. Can you do that?"

"Yeah," Baglio said and felt a sense of relief that he would be spared.

"When he meets you in Hell, tell him Garrett said 'Fuck you.'" Franklin then dug the knife into Baglio's artery, severing it in two, and quickly put a pillow over his head until he stopped moving.

More banging on the door. "Open this fucking door or I'll break it down!" the voice behind the door yelled.

Franklin took the white coat and the mask off and put them on the bed. He unlocked and opened the window and stepped onto the fire escape. He climbed down three stories to the street. Slowly he walked to the front of the building where he had parked his car and drove to the University of Pennsylvania Hospital to visit Mercy.

When Franklin arrived, Jacob was in Mercy's room. "How is she?" Franklin asked.

"Ask her yourself. She's awake," Jacob said.

"Mercy, how are you baby?" Franklin asked.

"I'm okay, Uncle Frank. It hurts though," Mercy answered.

"I know it does, baby, but it'll get better. You know I was shot in the leg," Franklin said, pointing to a spot on his leg. "It's fine now."

"Who shot you, Uncle Frank?"

"A German soldier. It was in the war."

"Did German soldiers shoot me?"

"No, honey. It was a couple of crazy men. Don't worry. They're gone now and can't hurt you anymore."

Jacob looked at Frank and motioned with his head to meet outside. "Mercy, Uncle Frank and I need to talk a minute. You rest and we'll be right back," Jacob said.

"Okay, Papa. Papa, did you think about our old house?" Mercy asked.

"Not yet, but I promise I will," Jacob said. "Now rest for a few minutes."

Jacob took Franklin's arm and guided him to the hall. "What'd you get, Frank?

"Chicago mob did it."

"Yeah, our guy told us that too," Jacob said.

"I got a name."

"Adone. Right?" Jacob asked.

"Right."

"Anything else?" Jacob asked.

"He's at the *Bellevue-Stratford* Hotel. At least that's where the shooters met him," Franklin said.

"Good. Let's have Mike check to see if he's registered."

"Okay," Franklin answered. "By the way, what was Mercy saying about the old house?"

"That kid is something. She's shot up and hurting, but still she is thinking about the welfare of other people," Jacob said with pride.

"How so?"

"She was asking what we were doing with the old houses on Wishart Street. She thinks it would be nice to let homeless people live in them. What a heart that kid has," Jacob said.

"Ha! That might not be a bad idea. We can't sell them until things get better. They're just going to sit there and gather dust. It couldn't hurt our community image. Amato is always getting press for helping the Italian community. Why can't we do the same?" Franklin asked.

"I'll put some numbers together. See what it will take. Right now we have more important things to do," Jacob said.

"I'll go see Mike," Franklin said as he patted Jacob on the shoulder and walked off.

14

"Adone flew the coop," Mike said.

"Any idea of where he went?" Franklin asked.

"He had the hotel clerk mail a package to a Chicago address," Mike answered.

"What's the address?"

"The clerk couldn't remember, but he said it was addressed to Angelo Adone. He thought that was kind of odd, to send a package to yourself," Mike said.

"Mike, get some feelers out and find out where Adone lives in Chicago. The hotel probably has his address," Jacob said.

"Will do."

Franklin left Mike and returned home for a shower and something to eat. Then he walked over to Jacob's house to give him a report.

"We'll find him, Jacob, and when we do it won't be pleasant," Franklin said.

"We can't seem weak Frank. These Chicago assholes are animals and only understand power. We need to find out what they're up to and if they are working with someone here in Philly. We need to make an impression," Jacob said. "And we need to make Adone pay."

"We'll teach them not to fuck with our families," Franklin said. Then after a pause, he asked, "When do the docs say Mercy can come home?"

"A day or two more, just to be sure there is no infection. She's doing good," Jacob said.

The doctor told Jacob that Mercy's arm was healing nicely, but that she would probably have numbness and mobility issues for the rest of her life. Exercise might help, but she should be prepared to cope with this disability.

"I've decided to turn our old homes into temporary housing for the poor like Mercy wants," Jacob said.

"It's a good idea, Jacob. It can help build a positive image for us. Who'd you have in mind to run it?" Franklin asked.

"Why—you want the job?"

"Fuck no. That would bore me to death," Franklin replied, laughing.

"I was thinking of asking Rose if she would lead the effort. She can get Graham to help," Jacob said.

"Perfect. Have you told her yet?"

"I talked to her. She likes the idea but is worried that she won't be able to take care of our house. I told her I would hire someone and she could supervise. She liked that," Jacob said.

Franklin laughed. "I bet. She's got plenty of experience bossing us around."

"Keep this to yourself for now. I want to surprise Mercy. I have to get to the hospital. Come by later if you have any news."

Jacob drove to the hospital, followed by Grady and a couple of his men. He had an odd feeling in his gut. He was concerned about the attempts on his life and the impending war, but he was also excited. It was a kind of an exhilaration he had not felt in a long time. He thought he saw the same excitement in Franklin and wondered why many men seemed to get a kick out of participating in dangerous things. He had read a book once about ancient Rome and the legions that had conquered the world. Above all, they believed in honor and glory. To have one's name be honored for thousands of years was the biggest prize. Was that why he was excited about this war or was it really only to protect his family?

When Jacob arrived at the hospital, he checked in on Mercy and she seemed to be much better. After about an hour, Mercy fell asleep.

"Molly, I have to make a phone call. Be back in a few minutes," Jacob said.

"Jacob, are we at war again? I don't know if I can take it again," Molly said in despair.

"It'll be okay, Molly. I'll take care of everything. How about you and the kids go to Cape May for a few weeks? That's if the doctors allow Mercy to travel," Jacob suggested.

"I don't want to leave you," Molly implored.

"The sea air will be good for Mercy, and it'll give me time to deal with the people that did this to her. I want you and the kids safe," Jacob said.

"Okay," Molly agreed, realizing her first duty was to keep the children safe.

"You can leave as soon as the doc says it's okay. Brian and a couple of his boys will take you and stay until I come get you, okay?" Jacob said

"Okay Jacob, but please be careful."

"I will," Jacob said. "I'll go make that call now. Be back in few minutes."

Jacob dreaded making this call. He liked Amato, a man who had become as much a mentor as a business partner. Much of what Jacob had learned about organizing and running his gang he had learned from Amato. He enjoyed their discussions about Italian history and politics, and the stories of the various Popes. He especially enjoyed the stories about Niccolò Machiavelli, a diplomat and writer during the Renaissance. At Amato's suggestion, Jacob even read a book Machiavelli wrote. Amato often had dinner with Jacobs' family when his father was alive. Amato and the older Byrne actually enjoyed each other's company and spent hours talking about the old days.

Jacob was very much afraid that Amato might have had something to do with the attempts on his life. If he did, Jacob would have to kill him. That would be difficult, but he would do it nonetheless.

Jacob dialed Amato's number and got one of his henchmen instead. "Is he there?"

"Yeah. Who's this?" the man asked.

"Byrne."

"Hold on."

After a minute, Jacob heard Amato's voice. "First, you tell me how my bella bambina Mercy is doing?"

"She's doing good, Don Amato. Doc says she'll be out of the hospital soon," Jacob said.

"Thank God," Amato said *as* he made the sign of the cross, kissed his fingers, and pointed to Heaven.

"Thank you. She really liked the doll you brought her when you visited," Jacob said.

"It's from Italy; a puppet. His name is Pinocchio. It's from a story about a puppet who turns into a boy and whose nose grows bigger when he lies. My mama, may she rest in peace, used to read it to me when I was a boy," Amato said as he made the sign of the cross again.

"Don Amato, I have an important question for you. And when you answer I hope your nose does not grow," Jacob said.

"I'm disappointed. Have I ever lied to you, Jacob?"

"No, and you know I trust you, but the men who tried to kill me and who hurt Mercy were Italians."

"Not my Italians. You tell me who they are and I'll make sure they never see another sunset," Amato said angrily.

"No need; the shooters are dancing with the devil as we speak," Jacob said.

"Good. I swear to God and on my children's lives that I had nothing to do with this," Amato said and made the sign of the cross once again.

"I believe you," Jacob said. As religious as Amato was he would never swear on his children's lives for fear that God would take his kids if he broke his word. Jacob was relieved to a point, but he was not 100% convinced.

"What did you learn from these men?" Amato asked.

"They were hired by the Chicago mob. A guy named Angelo Adone. You know him?" Jacob asked.

"I met him. He's an enforcer for Nitti."

"We think he's back in Chicago now," Jacob said.

"Jacob, please stop. I cannot hear this. I've told you about this commission my people have set up. They have the power now. If I betray them, they send some Jews down from New York and that's it for me and my sons.

"Don..." Jacob started, but was interrupted by Amato. "Please, just let me finish. I can talk to Luciano and the other commission members and see if I can make this threat go away, but it will take some time."

"Thank you, Don Amato. I appreciate any help you can give. But I have to tell you I am going to kill Adone and then Nitti," Jacob said.

"Jacob, please! If you kill Nitti, I will be able to do nothing. You will have a war you cannot win. Please reconsider," Amato said, wringing his hands.

"Adone is a dead man. I'll think about Nitti. I need to know why they want us out of the way. I think they must be working with someone here in Philly. I need to know who. Can you help me with that?" Jacob asked.

"I will try to find out. If you have to kill Adone then do it, but leave Nitti alone. Adone was responsible for a family member being hurt and we have rules about not hurting innocents. I can explain Adone's killing, but I cannot do anything if Nitti is killed," Amato said with conviction.

"Thank you, Don Amato. I am sorry to have thought you might have had some connection to this. I should have known better," Jacob said.

"You were protecting your family and there is no more important job for a man," Amato said. "Tell Mercy her Pop Pop Amato will visit tomorrow. Maybe I will have a gift for you as well."

Jacob hung up the phone and shook his head to clear his thoughts. He wasn't totally convinced Amato wasn't involved. If Amato got him the Philly connection, that would be a good sign. He could, however, just be setting him up for an ambush. Jacob would have to find a better way to test Amato's loyalty.

As Jacob walked back to Mercy's room, her doctor saw him and asked if they could talk for a few minutes.

"Mr. Byrne, Mercy is doing very well. The wound looks like it will not be infected and there is no fever. I believe we can discharge Mercy tomorrow morning."

"That's great news, doc. I really appreciate what you and the staff have done for Mercy," Jacob said.

"That's our job, Mr. Byrne, and Mercy made it easy. She is a strong little girl."

"Doc, I was thinking of sending Mercy and my wife to the shore for a few weeks. Do you think Mercy can travel?" Jacob asked.

"That should be fine, but I want you to check in with a doctor when they get there. I want to keep an eye on the wound. Come by around eight in the morning and you can pick Mercy up."

"Thanks Doc," Jacob said as he shook the doctor's hand and then walked off to Mercy's room.

Mercy was awake again when Jacob entered the room. Franklin was also there with Molly.

"This kid's strong like Popeye, except she don't need spinach," Franklin said holding his arm up and closing one eye like the cartoon character. "She was just telling me she wants to start swimming because the doctor says it will be good for her arm."

"I think you'll have to wait until your wound is healed, but after that I'll arrange to get you lessons," Jacob said. "We could all do with some more exercise. How about I have a pool built in our backyard?"

"Oh yeah!" exclaimed Mercy. "I can swim every day. Can I have my friends over?"

"Sure," Jacob said. "I have some good news. The doctor said you can leave tomorrow morning."

"Is she okay to leave?" Molly asked, concerned.

"The doc thinks so; he wants us to bring her home tomorrow morning," Jacob said.

"Oh Mercy. did you hear that? You can go home in the morning!" Molly said as she kissed Mercy on the forehead.

"Tomorrow, Uncle Brian will drive everyone down to Cape May for a couple of weeks. The salt air will help you heal," Jacob said.

"Are you going, Papa?" Mercy asked.

"I'll come down later. I have some work to do now," Jacob said

"Mommy, can we go to the boardwalk in Wildwood?" Mercy asked excitedly.

"Of course."

"Yeah!"

"Mercy, Uncle Frank and I have some business to talk about. We'll be back in a few minutes," Jacob said as he took Franklin's arm and steered him to the doorway.

When they were clear of the room, Jacob asked, "Any word on Adone?"

"We got him. He's shacking up with his mistress at her apartment at 6590 South Shore Drive. Ritzy ass place," Franklin said.

"Any other places he hangs out?"

"He has a house with his wife and kids in the Lincoln Park area. But he hasn't been there since we've been tracking him," Franklin said.

"Okay. Can you arrange to get four tickets to Chicago for tomorrow night?" Jacob asked.

"Sure. But why four tickets?" Franklin asked.

"I promised Graham," Jacob said.

"Gotcha."

The next morning Jacob called Don Amato.

"Good morning, Don Amato."

"Good morning, Jacob."

"I wanted to let you know Mercy is leaving the hospital this morning. Doc says she's doing great."

"That's good news, Jacob. I'll stop by the house to see her," Don Amato said.

"I'm sending the kids and Molly away today for a while. I don't want them around if trouble starts," Jacob said.

"That is good. If there's anything I can do, let me know. Do you need men to look after them?" Don Amato suggested.

"I appreciate your offer but I have it covered," Jacob said.

"Okay. I have some information for you," Don Amato said. "Adone is working with a numbers guy here in Philly named Herman Schulz. He's a fucking heini. You know him?"

"I know him," Jacob said, gritting his teeth. "He's one of the numbers guys we took over earlier a couple months ago. That fucking prick. I'll deal with him. Thank you Don Amato."

"I'm happy to help," Amato said.

"By the way, we found Adone. He has a house in Lincoln Park. We're going to hit him in two days."

"Stop. Tell me no more. Do what you have to do, but stay away from Nitti," Amato said firmly.

Jacob had told Amato the Lincoln Park location because they were going to hit Adone at his mistress's house on South Shore Drive. If Amato was working with Adone he would warn him and Adone would put guards on the house and probably try to set up an ambush. Jacob would have some men watching the house. If the ambush was set up then Amato had betrayed Jacob.

"Okay. I hope Mercy and the family can come home in a couple of weeks. Can you visit then?" Jacob asked.

"Yes, of course. I will look forward to seeing my angelo bella then," Amato said.

Accompanied by four men, Jacob, Molly and Mercy left the hospital for home.

As they passed by the old Byrne mansion and continued north on Broad Street, Mercy asked, "Papa? I thought we were going home."

"I have one stop to make first. Then we'll go home," Jacob said.

Ten minutes later, the car stopped on the corner of Wishart Street— across from Jacob and Franklin's old residence.

Mercy smiled brightly. "Oh! I love our old house. Are we going in?" Mercy asked.

"Maybe, but I want to show you something first," Jacob said as he helped her out of the car. Molly, Mercy and Jacob crossed the street and stood on the northeast corner. "Can you read the plaque, Mercy?"

"What's a plaque?" Mercy asked.

"It's a sign. See it up there?" Jacob asked, pointing to the heavy-set bronze embedded in the wall.

"Oh! It says Mercy."

"That's right. What about the rest?" Jacob asked.

"It says... 'Mercy Row. **People live in each other's shelter**.' Then it says, 'The Mercy Byrne Foundation.' What's it mean, Papa?"

"'**People Live in Each Other's Shelter**' is an old Irish saying and it means we are responsible to help each other out. I decided that you had a great idea in sharing our empty houses with the homeless. In your honor we have named it Mercy Row," Jacob said.

Mercy's mouth curled into a large smile and she hugged her father for what felt like hours. She then said, "Thank you, Papa. Thank you!"

Molly joined in the hug and the three of them shared a tender moment, with tears of happiness in their eyes.

15

Jacob, Franklin, Graham and Mike took the overnight train to Chicago. They had purchased sleeper car tickets but Jacob couldn't sleep. He wondered how the others could sleep like babies the night before a battle. There was no doubt in Jacob's mind that they were racing towards an unavoidable war and that the real battles would start after they took care of Adone.

The Chicago mob was well known for their violence. Back in 1927, a rival gang leader pissed off Al Capone off, so he lined seven of his men up against a garage wall and machine-gunned them to pieces. The only thing left alive in the garage was a dog and one of the men who had been shot twenty times. He died soon after. Capone was in jail for tax evasion but the killings continued. Some said Capone was still running the operation from jail through Frank Nitti.

To complicate things, the Italians had come up with this idea of having a commission. Each individual mob was represented and there was a Chairman. It was something like a corporation's board of directors. Their goal was to head off disputes between the gangs and stand together in strength. This is what worried Jacob most. He could fight Schulz, the guy the Chicago mob was in bed with in Philly. He probably could also fight the Chicago mob, but he could not fight all the Italian gangs. If Don Amato was in on this, Jacob knew that this would be the end for him, Frank and their business.

"Frank, wake up. We're almost there," Jacob said while shaking Franklin's arm.

"Whaaat? What the fuck, Jacob? You just fucked up a great dream," Franklin said groggily. "How much longer?"

"About two hours."

"Two fucking hours! And that's close?" Franklin asked.

"Yeah, we need to do some planning."

"Ok," Franklin said, shaking his head to clear it. "Let me go brush my teeth. Want me to wake up Mike and Graham?"

"No, let them sleep a while longer," Jacob said.

"Yeah, wake me up but let them sleep. Prick," Franklin said as he headed to the toilet. Jacob smiled.

When Franklin retuned, he and Jacob walked to the club car and ordered eggs, bacon, toast and black coffee.

"You in a better mood now?" Jacob asked Frank.

"Yeah, but you really did fuck up a good dream. I was in New York with three dames and..."

"Okay, Frank. I don't need the details. How are we getting in touch with the men watching Adone's house?" Jacob asked.

"When we get to Chicago I'll call their hotel. One guy watches the house while the other stays at the hotel. He'll go get an update and call us at our place," Franklin answered.

"I'm hoping for our sake, and his, that Amato is not involved. I like that old wop," Jacob said.

"Yeah."

Franklin and Jacob finished their breakfast and discussed plans for the hit on Adone. It was a sure thing that he would have bodyguards. They already knew about the guard at the front of the building and another at the rear. They didn't know how many were inside. There were only two exits from the tenth-floor apartment where Adone would be canoodling with his mistress. These were probably guarded as well, and there was perhaps another guard standing just outside the apartment door. Jacob guessed they would find out when they went in.

When they arrived in Chicago, the four men took a cab to their hotel and Franklin called his man covering Adone's house. While they waited for information, they ordered an early lunch from room service. Forty-five minutes later, Franklin's man called.

"Well, there's no activity at the Adone house. Everything seems normal. No guards," Franklin said.

"Good news. Keep our guy there until we leave," Jacob said.

"Already done."

"Good. We hit the mistress's apartment at midnight. Graham, you up for this?" Jacob asked.

"What the fuck do you think?" Graham snapped back.

"Okay, okay. Just asking," Jacob said.

"You don't have too. I want that fucking Ginzo," Graham said.

"Take it easy, Graham. Jacob's just asking. After all, you are getting a bit long in the tooth," Mike said, laughing.

Franklin looked at Jacob wide-eyed and smiled. "Oh shit!"

"You have no call to talk to me that way, Mike. I can beat your ass any day of the week and twice on Sunday," Graham said more calmly than Franklin thought he would.

"Oh yeah, Grandpop? You been drinking too much fucking whiskey if you think that is even a remote possibility. You old sod," Mike said.

"Okay, that's fucking it. You and me, Mike. Right now," Graham said as he took off his jacket and loosened his tie.

"You got it, Pops."

"Whoa guys! Let's cool it down. There's no need for this," Franklin said.

"You stay the fuck out of this, Frank," Graham said in an angry voice.

Franklin backed up and looked at Jacob, who tilted his head in a gesture that meant "there's nothing we can do."

Then Graham took a seat on one side of the table and Mike on the other side. They rolled up their right arm sleeves and grasped each other's hands, fingers to fingers.

"Ready," Graham said.

"Ready," Mike replied, as he tried to wrap his thumb around Graham's thumb.

The two men each tried to pin the others thumb down and if they succeeded and kept it pinned for the count of three they won the round. Graham won all three rounds.

"What the fuck was that?" Franklin asked in amazement.

"Thumb wrestling. Little Charlie showed us," Mike said.

"What? And you knew about this thumb wrestling?" Frank asked Jacob.

"Yeah."

"And you let me think they were going to kill each other?"

"Yeah," Jacob said, laughing. "Graham's the champ thumb wrestler. Nobody can beat him."

"Why have I never seen this before?" Franklin asked.

"Probably because you're always out fucking somebody's wife," Mike said.

"True," Franklin said. "Get up, Mike. Let me give this old fart a try."

The four men continued to thumb wrestle and then tried arm wrestling. In every case, Graham beat the younger men. After they all conceded that Graham was the champion of arm and thumb wrestling, they played poker. Jacob was glad for the diversion. It helped him control his jitters.

"Come on guys, it's almost eleven. Time to go. We have work to do," Jacob said.

The four men rose from the table and put their coats and ties on. Graham first strapped on his two-sided arm holster and placed a .45 automatic in each holster. The other men checked their weapons and they all departed for Adone's mistress's house.

When they arrived at the apartment, they parked on the street a block from the entrance. They walked halfway towards the building when a man came out from between two parked cars. Graham drew his gun.

"Take it easy. He's with us," Mike said. What's the deal, Tim?"

"He's still in there. Been there all day. Either he's a horny son of a bitch or he's scared shitless and hiding out," Tim answered.

"You positive?" Mike asked.

"Yeah, I saw him go in and he ain't come out yet. Pete's at the back and he ain't seen him neither."

"Okay, good job," Mike said. "We're ready."

Frank and Mike circled around to the rear of the building.

"Tim, can you handle the front door guard?" Jacob asked.

"Yeah," Tim answered.

Jacob told Tim to take off his hat and tie. He then rubbed some dirt on Tim's shirt and some on his face.

"Just go up to the guard, act drunk and ask for a light. When you're close enough, introduce him to this," Jacob said as he handed Tim the eight-inch stiletto Amato had given him years before. "Okay, go."

As Tim started down the street, Jacob looked at Graham and nodded. Graham grinned.

As Tim took the first step up the stairway, the guard asked in a menacing tone, "What the fuck you doing?"

"I need a light. You gotta light, buddy?" Tim asked, slightly slurring his words.

"Stay there. Here," the guard said as he threw Tim a box of matches.

Tim picked the matches up and shakily tried to light his cigarette. He struck several matches before he was successful. Leaving the box open, he threw the matches back to the guard being sure they only went halfway up the steps. When the matchbox hit the cement it spilled its contents on the stairs.

"You fucking **drunk**!" the guard shouted as he came down several steps to pick up the matches.

At the same time, Tim came up the steps, saying, "Sorry, buddy. Let me get them."

"Get the fuck back you..." He was interrupted as Tim collided with him.

Tim had drawn his stiletto and shoved the point through the guard's jaw and into the roof of his mouth. The man looked at Tim, surprised. In a split second, Tim wondered what he would look like when he died. He put both hands on the hilt of the knife and pushed the point into the man's brain. The guard fell forward, like a sack of potatoes, onto Tim. Both of them rolled down the steps and onto the pavement.

Jacob and Graham ran up and Graham pulled the guard off Tim.

"You okay?" Jacob asked Tim.

"Yeah, I'm good, but where's the blood? I thought there would be more blood," Tim said.

"What the fuck are you talking about? Get up," Graham said as he grabbed Tim by the shirt collar and hoisted him to his feet.

Jacob and Graham picked up the dead guard, took him to the landing, and put him sitting upright on a bench. Jacob placed his hat over his eyes.

"Tim, stay here and act like you're the guard. Put your tie back on and if anyone comes by and asks, he's sleeping off a drunk," Jacob said, pointing to the guard. "Let's go, George."

In the back of the building, Franklin and Mike met up with Pete and took down the rear door guard. Franklin left Pete at the back door and he and Mike worked their way to the lobby to meet Jacob and Graham. As they started to enter the lobby, they saw another guard at the elevator, who had seen them talking to the night deskman. He ran over, yelling at them. "What the fuck are you two doing?" He went for his gun.

Graham drew his weapon. At the same time, Mike ran up behind the man, dropped a garrote around his neck, and pulled. The man dropped the gun and tried to loosen the garrote with his index fingers. Mike pulled harder and the man fell backwards onto Mike, his legs flailing.

"Help me, will ya?" Mike said, grunting as he pulled the garrote tight.

Frank grabbed one side of the garrote and pulled as Mike pulled on the other side. The guard's eyes were protruding from his eyes, his tongue hanging long out of his mouth. Finally, he stopped moving and after a minute more, Mike and Franklin loosened their grips.

"Motherfucker. That guy's neck was thick," Mike said out of breath.

"Tell me," Franklin said, also out of breath.

"Put him in the other elevator and be sure it doesn't go up," Jacob said. "You. Come here," Jacob said, pointing to the night deskman.

The man had wet his pants and was wide-eyed as he approached Jacob. He shook his right leg to get out the urine.

"Y--yes sir?" the night deskman said, quivering.

"I know where you work. I can find out where you live. If you say any-thing you can be sure me or one of my gang will find you and you will get the same as him. Understand?" Jacob asked in a slow and deliberate voice.

"Yes sir," the man replied.

Jacob reached into his pocket, pulled out a roll of cash and peeled off two five-hundred dollar bills. He then handed them to the man. "Here. Take this for your trouble."

"But sir... these are McKinleys." the man said, amazed.

"Yeah! Well we gave you a lot of trouble," Jacob said, knowing that a thousand dollars was a year's salary for this man.

"Th--thank you, sir! Thank you," the man said as he was ushered out to the front door by Mike, where Tim was still standing guard.

When Mike returned, the four men started up the stairs to the third floor where Adone was staying with his mistress. The apartment was approximately ten doors down the hall and there was a guard posted by the door as expected. He was sitting on a chair to the left of the doorway, and he was brandishing a shotgun on his lap. There was no way to take the guard down without causing a commotion that would warn Adone that they were there. They would have to shoot the guard and rush the door, hoping Adone couldn't get to his gun before they got to him.

Mike crouched in the stairwell door, leaned out and fired three shots. One bullet hit the man in the head and he crumpled to the floor. Jacob, Frank and Graham rushed past Mike and ran for the apartment door. As they approached, five shots burst through the door, splintering the wood. Mike ran up, picked up the guard's shotgun, and blasted the door with two shots. The door lock was destroyed, and the shotgun blast had created a large hole in the middle of the door. Graham, Frank and Jacob opened fire through the door. When they stopped, they waited to see if there would be return fire. There was none. Mike pushed the door open with the butt of the shot-gun, while standing to the side. Two more shots rang out this time, coming through the wall where Mike was standing.

"Fuck!" Mike yelled as he realized he had been grazed in the arm.

Frank took a quick look through the hole in the door and motioned to Jacob that Adone was on the floor leaning up against the wall directly in front of them. Jacob leaned into the door and shot three times, hitting Adone once in the shoulder. Adone dropped his gun and screamed in pain.

Jacob burst through the door looking for anyone else who might be in the room. There was no one. He kicked the gun away from Adone's hand, then looked under the bed and saw that Adone's mistress was cowered in a fetal position and crying.

"We're not going to hurt you," Jacob whispered to her. "Just stay under the bed until we leave. And don't come out."

"You fucking bastards," Adone cried. "Do you know who I am?"

Graham entered the room casually, and walked straight over to Adone. He grabbed him by his neck and lifted him so he was eye-to-eye. "Yes, we know exactly who you are. You're the grease ball prick that shot my Mercy," Graham said as he increased the pressure on Adone's throat.

Adone began to kick wildly. He hit Graham in his side with his good arm, but Graham didn't seem to notice.

"Let me finish him," Mike said.

"No! I want to see the life leave his eyes," Graham replied.

Adone finally stopped thrashing and Graham let him drop to the floor. Then he said, "Now you can put one in his head."

Mike nodded grimly and aimed his gun right between Adone's eyes. He squeezed the trigger with as much interest as flicking off a light switch. The blast caused Adone's mistress to scream.

The three men left the room and casually walked to the stairwell. Jacob said, "Now we go back to Philly and visit Mr. Herman Schulz."

16

Mike's men had found Schulz holed up in a house in Fishtown, a section of the city with a large German and Polish population. After the failed attempt to kill Jacob, Schulz's men had abandoned him. They knew that the K and A Gang would retaliate and they would lose their livelihood, if not their lives. They made the claim of innocence to Jacob that they had not known about Schulz's alliance with the Chicago mob.

Jacob didn't believe them but in the interest of peace, and in getting his hands on Schulz, he allowed them to continue business as usual. The only difference was he placed one of his own men in charge of Schulz's crew.

"Mike, send a few guys to the house Schulz is held up in and bring him to the basement of 125 Wishart Street," Franklin said.

"You got it," Mike replied and left the room. Graham had gone to his room to clean up and get some sleep after he told Rose they were home.

"Here boys, I brought you something to snack on," Rose said as she placed a tray of fresh homemade oatmeal cookies on the table. "I have some coffee for you too,"

"Thanks, Rose. Have you heard from Molly?" Jacob asked.

"Yes she called when they arrived to let me know they were safe. She called again this afternoon to see if you were home yet. Molly said Mercy was doing very well. I have her number when you are ready to call her," Rose said.

"Thanks, Rose. I'll call her. First Frank and I have some more business to discuss and I need a bath," Jacob said.

"Okay then, I'll leave you two alone," Rose said as she left the room.

Franklin and Jacob discussed their plans for Schulz and decided they would call Amato after they took care of Schulz.

"These cookies are the best," Franklin said, his mouth half-full.

"Yeah, I see you like them a lot. You had five already. Better watch out or you may lose your manly physique," Jacob said.

"Nah, I get plenty of exercise," Franklin said.

"Yeah, doing pushups over some dame. I don't know how the women of Philadelphia got along while you were away for two days," Jacob said.

"Don't you worry, my boy. I'll make it up to them," Frank said, laughing.

"You do that, but first we have a little more work to do. For now I am getting a bath," Jacob said.

"Okay. I'll do the same and meet you back here in two hours," Frank said as he took several more cookies.

Franklin arrived at Jacob's house two-and-half hours later, delayed by the broad who had helped him bathe.

"Where the fuck have you been? You're late" Jacob asked impatient to take care of the Schulz situation.

"I had a little trouble with my bath. It got a little too hot."

"Okay. Let's go. What was her name?

"Who."

"Miss little too hot."

Franklin shrugged.

They then drove to the old house on Wishart Street.

They parked on Howard Street and took the alleyway to the house. Using the special doorway they had built, they entered the basement. There were still several old beer kegs in the large room and the coal furnace.

The basement had a faint odor of mold. Jacob had been careful to seal the walls and floors because they had stored their whiskies and beer there. Still the mold had worked its way in.

Jacob and Franklin sat down on some chairs that Mike had put in the room, and waited for Schulz to arrive.

"Did you talk to Molly?" Franklin asked.

"I did. She's fine, and Mercy is healing well," Jacob said.

"Did Molly ask about me?" Franklin asked.

"You fucking pervert. That's my wife you're talking about," Jacob said, laughing.

"I didn't mean that. You know better. I'm just fond of your family," Franklin said.

"I know, just yanking your chain. She did ask about you," Jacob said, still laughing.

"How's the hotel they're staying in?" Frank asked.

"She says it is beautiful. They've been to the beach, but it's too cold to go in the water."

"Well, it is October. That reminds me, the Eagles are playing the Giant's October 15th. Maybe we can take your boys to see them," Franklin said.

"Football? Nah. Baseball's my game," Jacob said.

"Well you're a week too late. The last game was Sunday, a week ago. They lost as usual and..." Franklin was interrupted when the basement door flew open and a body came rolling down the steps. Schulz slowly got to his feet, battered pretty badly. Blood was dripping from a wound on his head.

"Hey, Frank! Look who came to visit?" Jacob asked.

"Well I'll be. It's Mr. Schulz. Here, let me give you a seat," Franklin said as he grabbed Schulz by the lapels and threw him into one of the chairs. The chair fell backwards under Schulz's weight and he hit his head on the concrete floor.

"What the fuck, Frank! You knocked him out. Help me lift him up. We don't want him dead...yet," Jacob said. "Mike, keep two guys with you and tell everyone else to go home."

Franklin and Jacob lifted Schulz to a sitting position and slapped his face to wake him up.

"Verfickter Schwanzlutscher! Fick dich!" Schulz mumbled angrily.

"What'd you say, dick wad?" Franklin asked as he slapped Schulz again.

"I said, motherfucking cock suckers. Fuck you!" Schulz screamed.

"Leave him alone, Frank. I have a few questions," Jacob said as he saw Franklin ready to pounce.

"Okay, but I hope he doesn't answer you. I can't wait to make this guy scream some more," Franklin said.

Schulz looked at the two men, from Jacob to Franklin, asked, "What do you want?"

"Schulz, I already know you're working with the Chicago wops. So don't try to tell me otherwise. Adone is dead. The shooters are dead. They hurt my daughter and they paid," Jacob said in a calm voice.

"I didn't know they were going to try to hit you. I swear," Schulz said.

"I understand. The Italians come to town and tell you that you will work with them or you die. I get it. I know how much of a fucking bastard they can be. "Look, I have a question for you and if you answer it truthfully you can walk. Got it?" Jacob asked.

Schulz nodded his head slowly. "Yes."

"Who else was involved in this rebellion of yours?" Jacob asked.

"Just my second—Biermann. Adone said Nitti was okay with it," Schulz said.

"That's it? How about the Philly wops? They involved in this?" Jacob asked in a low and calm voice.

"No. Adone said I couldn't let anybody from the Philly mob know," Schulz said.

"Okay, good. That's all I have for you. Mike, will you take care of Mr. Schulz for me please?" Jacob asked.

Mike pulled his gun and walked over to Schulz.

"But you sai…" The bullet interrupted Schulz.

Schulz fell backwards and Mike leaned over him and shot another bullet into his forehead.

"Mike, get the guys to break up the concrete here and dig a hole. Then plant him in it. Make it deep. I don't want the smell coming up," Jacob said. "And find this guy Biermann and take him for a swim in the Delaware."

17

Jacob and Franklin drove back to the Byrne mansion. Graham was awake and they filled him in on what Schulz had said. Jacob grabbed the bottle of Irish whiskey from the table and poured three glasses. He held his glass up and said, "To my father. May he rest in peace." Graham poured some of the whiskey on the floor and both Franklin and Graham said, "Here, here."

Byrne's cat licked the whiskey up.

"Hey! Shoo, cat," Franklin said.

"No. it's okay. Shamus here is an Irish cat. He can handle his drink," Jacob said as he picked the cat up. "Can't you, Shamus?"

Jacob poured a small amount of whiskey in his glass and offered it to Shamus. The cat slurped it down. "My father used to give Shamus a thimble full of Irish whiskey every night. He said it made Shamus healthier."

"Well, you better pour me another before he drinks it all," Franklin said.

"One more and then we need to call Amato. I want to see if he knows anything about retaliation from Chicago," Jacob said as he poured three more glasses. They drank it down.

Jacob dialed Amato's number. There was no answer. He dialed again.

"Yeah?" a man answered.

"This is Byrne. Is Don Amato there?" Jacob asked.

"No."

"When will he be there?" Jacob asked.

"Don't know," the man replied.

"Can you tell him I called?"

"Yeah." The phone clicked off.

Jacob looked at the phone for a few seconds and hung it up. "Amato's man is a real chatterbox."

"What'd he say?" Franklin asked.

"Yeah. No. Don't know. Yeah," Jacob replied.

"Fucking wops," Franklin said.

Jacob poured three more whiskies. "Here's to a bright future in legit business."

"And not-so legit business," Franklin said.

"Here, here," Jacob and Graham said and the three downed their whiskey in unison.

The next morning the phone rang. Jacob was enjoying a simple breakfast of coffee and crumb cake with Rose and Graham. Rose answered the phone, and holding her hand over the receiver, asked, "Jacob, it's Don Amato. Are you home?"

"Yes, of course. I'll take it in the office."

Jacob took the seat behind his desk and picked up the phone. "Good morning, Don Amato."

"Buongiorno, Jacob. How is my Mercy doing?" Amato asked.

"Better. She's healing, but it could be a while before she can use her arm," Jacob said.

"I am happy she is getting better. I have heard that you, how shall we say, made things right?"

"News travels fast. Only one more to go," Jacob said.

"Please say no more," Amato pleaded.

"Okay, but what we say is between friends. Right?" Jacob said.

"Yes, of course. And, I have some news for you," Amato said.

"I am always happy to hear news from you, Don Amato" Jacob said as he shifted in his seat in anticipation.

"Yesterday I was in New York City at a meeting. Your name came up and I petitioned that this trouble between you and Chicago be worked out. I explained the attack on your daughter and it had the desired effect. But Chicago has always been less agreeable than the other organizations," Amato said and paused.

"So what does that mean?" Jacob asked

"I explained to them that we work together and that you are responsible for a large part of my revenue. I said that it would be disrespectful to me if they continued to pursue a course of action that would disrupt my revenue," Amato said.

"And?"

He told me vaffanculo madre su per il culo," Amato said.

"What's that mean?" Jacob asked, guessing that it wasn't something nice.

Amato straightened in his chair and said,"I cannot repeat it but it meant something like, 'Go fuck yourself'. I am afraid it made me lose my temper and the Chicago representative and I had a small scuffle," Amato said.

"How small?"

"I broke the asshole's nose," Amato replied.

"Are you in danger?"

"No. No one can put a hit on a boss without consequences. You, on the other hand..." Amato was interrupted by Jacob.

"I expected that," Jacob said. "We're ready for it."

"You don't understand. They won't stop until you're dead, unless I can work it out with the commission," Amato said.

"What's the likelihood of that?" Jacob asked.

"Good. They don't like how Chicago's been run. Too high profile. Pictures in the paper and all that. And with Capone in jail I think the commission will go my way. After all, they get a taste of what I make from our alliance. But it's going to take some time to get the commission in line," Amato said.

"How much time? I'm not sitting around to see what they do. I can go to Chicago and take care of Nitti myself," Jacob said.

"No! You cannot do that!" Amato said, pounding his fist on his desk. "If you do all the commission members will go after you. And that you cannot survive. Give me some time."

"Okay, okay. What can I expect?" Jacob asked.

"They'll send someone before I can get this fixed," Amato said.

"Who?" Jacob asked.

"I don't know. They like to use the guys in Detroit. Maybe someone from there," Amato said

"How about the New York shooters? Will they use them?"

"No. Siegel answers to the commission. They won't do it unless we lose the commission's trust. If that happens we both die," Amato said.

Jacob sat back in his chair, took a sip of coffee and said, "Well so be it. It's been ten years since we last had a war. Now I'm wiser and I have more money. We're ready."

"I'll do everything I can, but I cannot know your plans. If I hear who they are sending I'll let you know," Amato said.

"I appreciate that, Don Amato. When this is over, we'll get together. I'm sure Mercy would like to see her Pop Pop Amato," Jacob said.

"Soon I hope," Amato said as he made the sign of the cross and hung up the phone.

It had been three days since Jacob had talked to Amato and still no word on either the commission's decision or anything about who Chicago would send to kill him and Franklin. Jacob spent the time working on The Mercy Byrne Foundation, and plans to put homeless families in the houses on Wishart Street.

Jacob could place a family, maybe two, in each of the normal row homes. His and Franklin's homes could handle three families each and would be reserved for families with members who were ill. Each of these larger homes would have a caretaker and those caretakers would serve to keep an eye on the single-family homes as well. The construction costs would be minimal. All in all, it was working out well. He couldn't help thinking that Mercy, who had suggested this idea, was a special little girl and would grow up to be a very special woman.

Jacob couldn't sleep well and was up at 5 AM and he was wide awake. The last three days had been hell. He couldn't see his family and he was worried about them. He had no idea when Chicago would hit back. His nerves were on edge. Work always took his mind off his problems, so Jacob dug into the accounts for the new foundation.

It was about a half-hour after Jacob had woken up, while he was making some last entries in the accounting journal, when he heard shouting in the street. Then he heard gunshots. He immediately grabbed two guns and rushed to the entrance. Graham, who had heard the commotion, was already behind him, guns in hands. Looking out the doorway Jacob saw three men on Franklin's doorsteps and two of his men lying on the pavement. The men in the doorway were shooting at the men guarding Jacob's house who had taken cover behind his steps. Jacob fired several times. The assassins fired back. He ducked back in the doorway.

"We need to see what's happening around back," Jacob said.

"We already have men in the rear. I haven't heard any shooting," Graham said.

Jacob put his head around the door and saw the last of the three assassins entering Franklin's house. He ran out saying, "Fuck! They're in Frank's house. Let's go."

Graham was behind Jacob, and the two guards joined them. As they reached Franklin's doorway, several shots were fired at them. They fired back and entered the house. No one was in the entranceway.

"Frank's bedroom is on the second floor. You two go around to the back stairs and meet us up on the second floor," Jacob ordered. "George, let's go."

Graham and Jacob started up the stairs and heard several more shots. There was a scuffling from above and by the time Jacob and Graham made it to the bedroom it had stopped. They pushed open the door and burst into the room. No one was there. The bedclothes were in a pile and still smoking from where the bullets had pierced the fabric.

"Oh fuck… No! Frank!" Jacob yelled as he rushed to the bed.

Just as Jacob was next to the closet door, it slammed into him hard, knocking him to the floor. A man ran out and crashed head-on into Graham. Graham grabbed the man by the neck and a shot rang out. Graham dropped the man and he ran out of the room and down the steps. By the time Jacob was back on his feet, the man was gone and Graham was standing by the door with a shocked expression on his face. Jacob could see the red stain begin to spread on the cloth of Graham's shirt. Graham looked down, saw it, then fell to the floor. By the time Jacob got to him, Graham was dead.

Jacob kneeled by Graham and put his hand on Graham's forehead. He said his goodbyes and closed Graham's eyelids. Then Jacob looked at Franklin's bed and summoned the courage to see what they had done to Frank. He hesitated as he took the covers in his hand, not wanting to see. Not wanting to believe that Frank was gone also, he pulled the covers back.

18

No one was in Franklin's bed.

Rose was woken by the gunshots. By the time she arrived at the front door, the fighting was over and Jacob was standing on the front steps of Franklin's home. He was talking to several of his men. She heard sirens in the distance and decided to go see what was happening. When she was halfway to Franklin's house Jacob saw her and hurried to intercept her before she got there.

"Rose, let's go back to our house," Jacob said as he took her arm and guided her back.

"What's going on?" Rose asked in a worried voice.

"Some guys broke into Franklin's house," Jacob said.

"Oh my God! Is he okay?" Rose asked.

"Rose, I don't know. He's missing."

"Maybe he's just out?" Rose said with hope.

"I'm sure that's it."

"Where's George?" Rose asked.

"Here, let's get inside and I'll fill you in," Jacob said, avoiding her question.

Rose and Jacob entered the house and he motioned for her to sit on the sofa. He took a place next to her.

"Can I get you some coffee, Jacob?" Rose asked.

"No thank you, Rose," he said as he took her hand. "I have some bad news."

Rose sat motionless, staring at Jacob.

"Don't say it. Don't! Rose said as she pulled her hand away

"George is gone, Rose. He was shot."

Rose just sat, looking at Jacob for a few second. Then she fainted, falling back on the couch.

Jacob called the doctor and carried Rose to her room. He waited with her until the doctor arrived and then went back to Franklin's house and gave the police what information he knew, leaving out that they had been assassins. He told the police that it was a robbery attempt.

Two of Jacob's guards were injured and were taken to a nearby hospital. An ambulance took George to the coroner's office. Two of the assassins had been shot to death trying to get out the back of the house and they were also taken to the morgue along with the maid.

"The meat wagons are gone, Jacob," Mike said.

Jacob looked at his watch and couldn't believe it was already ten in the morning. "Where is Frank?" Jacob asked. Mike hunched his shoulders, indicating he didn't know.

"I'll get some guys looking for him," Mike said.

"Good."

Jacob walked back to his house and made a pot of coffee. He poured two cups and went to Rose's room. The doctor had sedated her and left a nurse to look after Rose for when she woke up. Jacob nodded to the nurse and offered her a cup.

"Thank you sir," the nurse said, taking the cup in two hands. "The lady's sleeping now. She'll be okay."

"Rose; her name is Rose," Jacob said.

"Sorry, sir. The doctor didn't tell me her name."

Jacob nodded again and left the room. He went down the stairs and to his office. As he began to take his seat, the front door burst open with a bang. Jacob grabbed the pistol he kept under the desk and pointed to the open office door.

'What the fuck's going on?" Franklin yelled as he entered the office.

"Jesus Christ, Frank! I almost shot you. Where the fuck have you been?" Jacob asked, heaving a sigh of relief and putting the gun away.

Jacob got up from behind the desk and walked over to Frank and hugged him. "We thought you were dead." Jacob released Frank and motioned for him to sit down.

"Saw Mike and Grady as I pulled up to the house. They gave me a quick rundown. Is Graham really dead? I can't believe it," Franklin said.

"The fucking guy shot him in the heart. One minute he was there and the next minute he's dead. I can't believe George is gone," Jacob said.

"Does Rose know?" Franklin asked in a low voice.

"Yes. I told her. She is in her room. The doc gave her something to make her sleep," Jacob said. "I'll call her daughters later and have them come over and be with her."

"Who did this?" Franklin asked in an angry voice.

"Who else?" Jacob answered.

"No… I mean, where are the shooters from?" Franklin asked.

"Don't know yet. Mike's got their wallets. Maybe we can trace them. One thing's for sure. They're not Italians," Jacob said.

Jacob called Molly to let her know what had happened. She wanted to rush back but Jacob told her it wouldn't be safe for her or the kids and that he hoped to have everything worked out in a few days. She could come back then.

It took until that early evening for Mike to get a lead on where the shooters were from and an address for their leader. Both men had driver's licenses with addresses in Oxford, Pennsylvania, a small town on the southeastern tip of Pennsylvania not far from the Maryland border. After a call to friends in Wilmington, Delaware, he was able to determine that they were probably part of a moonshine gang that operated out of the countryside between Oxford and Kennett Square. A family named Johnson ran the gang.

"Can we muster up fifty men?" Jacob asked Mike.

"Yeah, I can get fifty. When do you want them?" Mike asked.

"Now! I want to go to Oxford with an army to show these rednecks they shouldn't mess with us. I don't want to kill them, just scare them. These guys were not professionals and I think we can persuade them," Jacob said.

"What about the guy who shot Graham?" Franklin asked.

"He an exception. He dies tonight," Jacob said.

It was after one in the morning before Mike had the men ready. They lined twenty-four cars along Broad Street and waited for Jacob and Franklin. The trip would take approximately two hours, so it would still be dark when they arrived.

Jacob had called Don Amato to let him know Graham had been killed and to see what he knew about the men who had done it. Amato knew that the Chicago boys did some business with someone in Maryland but he didn't have any additional information. Amato promised to put more pressure on the commission to get Chicago to back off. He would go to New York again and talk to Luciano in the morning.

"Okay, Mike. You guys ready?" Jacob asked.

"We're ready. Baltimore Pike's the best way," Mike said.

"Lead the way then. Do the men know the plan?" Jacob asked.

"Yeah they know what to do. Grady and Brian will handle the stills," Mike said.

"Good. Let's go."

It was three in the morning when the convoy arrived at the Johnson farm. As soon as they pulled up, Grady and Brian went into the woods searching for the stills. It was likely there were several on them hidden in the forest, but they only needed one. While they were searching for the still Mike had the other men take positions surrounding the house.

It took an hour for Grady and Brian to find a still. It wasn't far from the house and was hidden in a ravine. There was only one person guarding the still and he was half-asleep, sitting on an old rocking chair. Grady silently came up behind him, picked up a large rock and smashed the man's head. He wasn't trying to kill the man, but it was clear from the crushed skull and brain matter on the rock that his efforts didn't work.

"Brian, get back over behind those boulders. This moonshine is gonna make a big bang," Grady said.

When Brian was safe behind the boulders, Grady took the two grenades from his pockets, pulled the safety pins and threw them at the still. Then he ran as fast as he could to the boulders. When he was almost there, the grenades went off, ignited the moonshine, and exploded. The concussion picked Grady up and threw him over the boulders. He landed several feet back from where Brian was crouching.

"Holy shit! You alright, Grady?" Brian asked as he checked his brother for blood and broken bones.

"Get the fuck off of me. I'm okay," Grady said. The two men looked at each other and laughed.

When Jacob heard the explosion, he opened the door to his car and stood beside it in the dark. The people inside the house had heard the explosion, scuffled to get their rifles, and rushed out the door to see what had happened. As soon as they did, Jacob told Frank to turn the car lights on. Like a Christmas tree, lights came on from all the cars surrounding the house. The brightness blinded Old Man Johnson and his two sons.

"Put the rifles down and tell everyone in the house to come out," Jacob yelled.

"Fuck you, revenuer!" Old Man Johnson yelled.

"We're not the law. We're the guys you tried to kill yesterday," Jacob yelled back.

"Drop the rifles. I have fifty men surrounding your house. We're not here to hurt you or your family. We just want to talk," Franklin said.

"Talk about what? We got nothing to say to you," Old Man Johnson said.

"If you don't drop your weapons and get the rest of the people out of your house we're going to shoot you and your sons and blow the house the fuck up with your family in it. Now don't be a stupid hillbilly," Franklin said.

Johnson motioned to his sons to drop their rifles and he did the same. He sent one of his sons in the house to get the other family members out. Two of Jacob's men picked up the rifles and brought the old man to Jacob.

"I'm showing you my face because I know you are not stupid enough to tell the authorities. I am sure you don't want them snooping around here," Jacob said.

The old man looked at him with contempt, but said nothing.

"Yesterday, three or more of your guys came to my city, to my home, and tried to kill me and Frank. As you can see, they didn't succeed; but they did kill one of our family members. Frank wants me to kill you, your sons and every man in your hillbilly gang."

The man looked alarmed.

"But I don't want to do that. I want the man who pulled the trigger. I want my vengeance, but if it can't be him then it will be you and your sons. Understand?" Jacob said in a slow and low tone.

"Fuck this. Just kill them and get it over with. I have a date tonight. I don't want to be here all day," Franklin said.

"What do you say, Johnson? It's you and yours or the man who did the deed," Jacob said, ignoring Frank.

"Okay, Okay. He lives in Oxford. I can send one of my sons to get him," Johnson said.

"Mike, take a couple of guys and go with... Which son are you sending?" Jacob asked Johnson.

"Caleb," Johnson said. "Caleb, come here."

Johnson told Caleb what to do and Mike and three others took Caleb to a car and drove off to Oxford. Jacob told Johnson to go back to his family and sit on the porch until Caleb returned.

The sun was just coming up when Mike returned with Caleb and Graham's murderer. He had his hands bound behind him and a hood over his head. Mike pulled him out of the car and pushed him towards Jacob. The man fell at Jacob's feet. Jacob motioned Mike to pick him up and Mike and Frank took him by the arms and stood him before Jacob.

"Take the hood off," Jacob said.

Mike took the hood off, revealing the man's face. He had a swollen bloody eye.

"Didn't want to come, huh?" Jacob asked.

"Caleb here convinced him," Mike said, nodding at Caleb.

Jacob took the man's face in his hands and said, "Yesterday you killed a very, very dear friend of mine."

"I didn't kill nobody."

"I might believe you, you stupid fuck, except you're still wearing the same clothes," Jacob said as he grabbed his shirt where the gun powder stain had blackened it.

"Frank, give me your tie," Jacob said.

"Come on Jacob, this is a silk tie," Frank replied. Jacob stared at Frank for a couple seconds, saying nothing. "Fuck." Frank took the tie off and handed it to Jacob.

Jacob took the tie and stuffed it in the man's mouth. The man started to run and Mike hit him on the back of the head, knocking him to the ground.

"Careful, Mike. We don't want to kill him…yet," Jacob said. "Get the rope. There's a good tree over there."

"Johnson, get your wife and the little ones in the house. Tell them to go to the bedroom and stay there," Frank said. "You and your sons stay here."

Jacob's men tied a loop in the rope and threw it over the tree. Mike put the noose around the man's neck and looked at Jacob.

"Mr. Johnson, I don't want to ever see you, or any of your family or gang in or near Philadelphia. You're done working with the Chicago mob. Do you understand this?" Frank asked.

"Yes," Johnson replied.

Frank took him by the shoulder and said, "Good, because if you don't do it, this is what will happen to you and your sons," Franklin said and nodded to Mike.

Four of Mike's men pulled on the rope and as the noose tightened, the man began kicking violently. Jacob allowed him to dangle for a minute or so and he pulled his .45 and emptied the clip into the man's chest. Mike's men dropped the man to the ground and Frank motioned everyone back in their cars. The convoy started back to Philadelphia. Old Man Johnson fell to his knees, his hands covering his face.

Frank and Jacob didn't say anything for thirty minutes while they were driving back to Philadelphia. Finally, Frank said, "Had to be done, Jacob. If we didn't do something they wouldn't stop."

"I know, Frank; I'm just glad he gave the man up. I didn't want to kill his sons," Jacob said.

"That was a pretty good bad-guy, good-guy routine. I make a good bad-guy," Frank said.

"You're a regular James Cagney, you are," Jacob said.

"I was thinking George Raft, but Cagney will do," Frank quipped.

19

Two days after Graham's murder, Jacob and Franklin took on the task of arranging Graham's burial. Jacob had thought they should lay him to rest near his father at Arlington Cemetery, but Rose wanted him buried Catholic, so they had decided on Holy Sepulcher.

"How is it Graham can be buried in Holy Sepulcher? He wasn't what I would call a good Catholic," Franklin asked Jacob.

"Apparently he went to church every week with Rose and even did confession a few times a year," Jacob said.

"Go figure," Franklin mused.

"I was thinking we should have a proper Irish wake tomorrow night before the burial. I think Graham might have liked that," Jacob said.

"You know I like a party more than anyone, but I could never figure out why when someone dies the Irish get drunk and party," Franklin said.

"My father told me that it's our way to celebrate the person's life and to give them a good send off. That's what I want to do for George," Jacob said.

"I'll make the arrangements. Where should we lay out George?" Franklin asked.

"My office. People can pay their respects and if it's like other wakes I've been to, the men will find their way to the kitchen close to the food and booze. The women will hover around Rose and try to comfort her," Jacob said.

"I'll go take care..." The phone suddenly rang, interrupting Franklin. "Maybe it's Amato," Franklin said.

Don Amato had traveled to New York to negotiate a peace between the Chicago mob and Jacob's gang. Earlier attempts had not worked and there was no good reason to believe his newest effort would work either.

"Hello?"

"Jacob! How are you?" Amato asked.

"Fine, Don Amato. How about you?" Jacob said.

"Good, Jacob, I am good. How's my Mercy?" Amato asked.

"She is doing much better. I'm hoping I can bring her home soon," Jacob said.

"That is wonderful. Please kiss her for me. How's Rose?" Amato asked.

Jacob often got frustrated with the way Italians had to get all the pleasantries out of the way before they would discuss business, no matter how important the business was.

"She's recouping, Don Amato. Everyone else is good. How's your family?" Jacob asked.

"They are also are good. My son Anthony has been helping me and when I die,"

Amato made the sign of the cross, "he will take over," Amato said with pride.

"Tony is a very capable man and will do you proud, but we are hoping Don Amato will be around for a long time," Jacob said.

Franklin mouthed the words, "What the fuck?" in an attempt to get Jacob to ask the burning question.

"Thank you, Jacob. I don't plan on going anywhere soon," Amato said with a chuckle.

"Don Amato, how was your trip to New York?" Jacob asked. Franklin threw his hands in the air in an act of triumph.

"As you can imagine, Nitti was not happy with my proposal. But I was finally able to convince the commission that it was in their best financial interest to broker a peace. They gave Nitti a choice. Have peace, or if he still wanted to kill you, he had to pay me for my losses to date and for an additional two years. When I told him how much that would be he quickly decided that peace was the best policy," Amato explained.

Jacob held his thumb up to Franklin and said, "That is good news. How can I ever repay you?"

"Jacob, I know that if I or my son ever needs your help you will provide it. That's all the pay I require. That and for us to continue to do business together," Amato said.

"You know you have my loyalty and so does your son," Jacob said.

"There may be one small problem. Nitti had sent two men to Philadelphia to kill you. This was, of course, before our agreement. Probably when he learned the hillbillies had failed. He said he would try to recall them but was not sure he could contact them before they acted," Amato said.

"Well we will hope Nitti can contact them. But if he doesn't—we'll be ready," Jacob said.

Jacob had felt the elation of knowing the war was over and then the let down when he learned he might have to fight one last battle. When the war first started, he had that twinge of excitement many soldiers get just before a battle. But losing Graham, the blood he had spilled, and missing his family all turned the excitement into disillusionment and fear. Fear that he might never see Molly and the children and disillusionment in a business that took so much from you. He vowed to himself that once this was all over he would turn the rackets over to Frank and just concentrate on the construction business.

"Amato convinced them," Jacob told Franklin after hanging up with Amato.

"Great. Now we can get back to making money," Franklin said in relief.

"There is one problem."

"Oh? What problem?" Franklin asked.

20

Franklin was pleased. George was in a beautiful cherry wood casket with brass and bronze fittings. He had placed George's two favorite guns under the pillow below his head and a bottle of the best Irish whiskey by his side. Franklin didn't believe that he would need any of this, or for that matter, that there was an afterlife. It just seemed like the right thing to do.

The coffin was in the middle of Jacob's office to allow visitors to move easily into and out of the room to pay their respects. Rose was sitting next to the coffin and her daughters were close by. Molly was sitting on her left side, holding her hand. Molly had refused Jacob's pleas not to come home until he was sure it was safe. He finally agreed, knowing she would never forgive him if she missed George's funeral. To Jacob's relief she did agree to leave the kids in Cape May with a nanny and several of his best men.

Neighbors and friends had been filing in and out of the room for hours and there didn't seem to be an end to the line of people still waiting to pay their respects to George Graham. Every mourner was searched before they entered the house. There were also guards on the back and front doors, in the alleyway behind the house, and on the street in front of the house. Jacob and Franklin were taking no chances while Nitti's men were still in town gunning for them.

Just as Jacob had predicted, the men who had come to celebrate George's life were congregated in the kitchen, getting drunk and telling stories about Graham, and the women were in the living room gossiping. Some of Rose's close friends were in Jacob's office, which had been opened for extra space.

Jacob stayed close to the door and greeted each mourner as they entered. He thought of the time at his mother's wake, when he and his father had done the same. And, he remembered during his father's wake the numbness he felt to the perfunctory words of sympathy from the visitors. But there was one person whose words he would never forget. Don Amato's.

Amato had told him there was nothing worse than losing your mother or father, except losing a child or wife. He said, "Jacob, it's okay to cry, to grieve for your father. Show your love—grieve, and when you can stop grieving, start living again. That is the best way to honor him."

Irish men were taught from a young age that men didn't cry. To cry was to show weakness. Women cried, children cried. Men did not. "What a fucking crock of shit," Jacob thought.

He couldn't help but admire the Italians. They were able to show their emotions, good or bad, and somehow he thought that gave them some peace of mind. It made them stronger.

"Frank. Take over here, will you?" Jacob asked. Then he went to the bathroom and cried. He cried for his mother, he cried for his father, and he cried for George. Mostly he cried for the man he had become and the realization that he would always be that man.

Graham's funeral procession was fifty cars long. It might have been larger but some of the men had stayed up all night drinking and were now sleeping it off. Their wives had to find rides with their friends.

Jacob and Frank were in a car with Rose and Molly. The trip was almost an hour long and everyone was excruciatingly silent. Rose cried soft tears most of the way and Molly consoled her. Frank would have liked to tell stories about Graham, but most of his memories were filled with violence and he didn't think that it would be appropriate. After all, Rose only knew him as a kind and caring man.

Frank had always maintained some fear when around Graham. When he had first met him—when Graham had come to the jail to pick the two up all those years ago— his fear was well warranted. However, in later years when he and Jacob worked with Graham, they had become close. Graham was a violent man and had punished men who crossed Jacob or his father with impunity. When he met and married Rose, he became a different person. He still was capable of murder, but outwardly, he had become gentle, even warm. Especially to Jacob's children.

"Frank, we're here." When Jacob didn't hear a response', he asked, "You sleeping?"

"No, just thinking," Franklin replied.

"I thought I smelled wood burning."

Mike had men placed discreetly around the cemetery grounds and armed guards were driving several of the cars in the procession. This was no time to let their guard down.

"Rose, here; take this seat," Jacob said, pointing to the middle of three chairs placed by the gravesite. Then he ushered Molly to Rose's left chair.

Don Amato arrived next and Jacob asked him to sit in the third chair. As Amato sat, he took Rose's hand into his and offered his condolences.

George's casket was placed on the straps that covered the open hole over the grave. Thirty reeves of flowers had been placed at the head of the grave. To the left of the reeves there was a Marine honor guard of seven men. All were dressed in their formal uniforms and each carried a rifle. Four of the men detached themselves from the group and took a place at the four corners of the casket.

Molly squeezed Rose's hand and said, "Rose, I didn't know George had been in the military."

"Yes, he was a sergeant during the Spanish-American War. That's where he met Jacob's father. He didn't like to talk about it but he did say he was with the force that took Guantanamo Bay. Other than that he didn't discuss it," Rose said.

"Well it's nice that he will be remembered for his service to the country," Molly said.

The priest began the ceremony by reciting, "I am the Resurrection and the Life," after which the four Marines removed the flag and folded it. A Marine officer then presented the flag to Rose.

The casket was slowly lowered into the grave and the priest recited the Canticle of Zachary, after which he sprinkled holy water on the casket. He then recited a final prayer. "Grant this mercy, O Lord, we beseech Thee, to Thy servant departed, that he may not receive in punishment the requital of his deeds who in desire did keep Thy will, and as the true faith here united him to the company of the faithful, so may Thy mercy unite him above to the choirs of angels. Through Jesus Christ our Lord. Amen." This was followed by, "May his soul and the souls of all the faithful departed through the mercy of God rest in peace."

Then taps was played, after which the first volley of seven shots was fired. Then the Marines loaded their rifles and fired the second volley. The Marines reloaded for the next volley and lifted their rifles to the sky. Amato was the first to see one of the marines lower his rifle and point it towards Jacob who was standing behind Molly. In a split second, he knew what was going to happen. Amato jumped from his chair to protect Rose and Molly as he yelled, "Gun!"

The Marine next to the man who had lowered his rifle pushed the long barrel of his gun high but he was too late. The gun had already gone off. The assassin dropped the rifle, pulled a revolver from his waistband, and shot the Marine in the head. He then ran off towards a large clump of woods about a hundred yards away as the Marine fell to the ground, blood spurting from the hole in his head.

There was pandemonium as people rushed to their cars and safety, wailing in fear.

"Alberto, take Rose and Molly to the car," Amato ordered. When they were gone, he said, "Anthony, please help me sit down."

"Are you okay, Don Amato?" Jacob asked.

"I have been shot," Amato said, incredulous.

"Let's get him to a hospital," Anthony said in panic as he grabbed his father to pick him up."

"Wait!" Amato commanded.

"Pop," Anthony implored.

Amato held his hand up to Anthony and said to Jacob, "Remember our deal, Jacob. If my son needs you, you will be there for him."

"Of course, Don Amato. I'll be there. Let's get you to a hospital," Jacob replied.

Jacob and Anthony picked up Amato and placed him in his car. Anthony told the driver to get them to the closest hospital and they drove off.

21

When Franklin saw the assassin running towards the trees he imme-diately took off after him. The assassin, seeing that he was being followed, wildly shot several rounds at Franklin, missing him entirely. Frank-lin pulled his revolver and shot back, but trying to shoot someone while you're running is virtually impossible. As Franklin closed on the assassin, the man stopped, spun around and pointed the pistol at him. Franklin tackled the man before he could fire and as they both fell to the ground Franklin's revolver was knock out of his hand.

The assassin struggled as Franklin grabbed the man's gun to prevent him from shooting. They rolled several times, each hitting the other with their free hand. As they rolled on the wet grass, Franklin was able to pull his knee upwards and into the man's groin. The assassin groaned and loos-ened his grip on the gun, giving Franklin a momentary opportunity to grab it out of his hand. As Franklin pulled the pistol away, the man pushed up and heaved Franklin backwards.

Franklin rolled once, now free of the assassin. The assassin quickly pulled a knife from his boot and lunged right at Franklin. Franklin raised the pistol and shot. The assassin twisted in the air as the bullet hit the side of his head. He landed on Franklin facing backwards as his blood and brains splat-tered on Franklin's face.

Franklin pushed the man off and without hesitation, ran towards the trees where he was sure he would find the assassin's partner. The clump of trees was small and in seconds, he pushed through to see the distinctive back end of a black Hupmobile racing down the road. He shot until he ran out of ammunition. Franklin threw the pistol on the ground in frustration and yelled, "Fuck!" as the car continued down the road, unmolested.

Suddenly, another car came pulling out of the cemetery grounds and T-boned the Hupmobile hard, knocking it well off the road. Franklin heard the crash and started running towards the steaming wreck. As he approached the scene, the driver who had crashed into the assassin pushed his door open and ran up to where the assassin lay unconscious over the steering wheel. It was Mike.

"Is he dead?" Franklin asked.

"No, just sleeping," Mike answered.

Franklin looked at the tracks Mike's car had made. They stretched into the cemetery lawn.

"How the fuck did you do that?" Franklin asked, pointing at the car.

"Borrowed it. I figured the fastest way to get back here was to drive across the cemetery. I saw the car peeling out and figured it was the guy's backup, so I hit him," Mike said.

"How'd you miss the grave stones?" Franklin asked.

"I didn't."

"Oh fuck! Now you are really going to Hell," Franklin said, laughing. "Whose car was it?" Franklin asked, pointing at the smashed front end of the car.

"Bishop Ryan. His driver was a little hesitant about me borrowing the car, but I reasoned with him," Mike said with a smile.

"Well, Mike my boy. This one's going to cost us a pretty penny in donations," Franklin said, smiling. Mike shrugged his shoulders.

Grady pulled up as they were dragging the driver out of the car. "Grady, get this prick back to the Wishart Street house. Put him in the basement. Don't hurt him… yet," Franklin ordered.

"You got it boss," Grady said. He waited while Franklin and Mike threw the man in the backseat of the car.

"I'll meet you there," Franklin said to Grady. I need to go see if Jacob's okay first."

22

Anthony Amato paced the waiting room floor, waiting for the news about his father's condition. His mouth was dry and his mood dangerous. His father had taught him to be calm during crises, but this was his pop. How could be calm? Nothing his father had taught him prepared him for this. For his father's death. If he did die, Anthony would be boss and he was not sure he could live up to the job.

Jacob and Franklin saw Anthony before he saw them.

"Tony," Jacob said as he touched Anthony's shoulder.

Anthony spun around in a defensive stance. "Oh, Fuck! Sorry, Jacob. I 'm wound up."

I understand, Tony. No need to apologize."

"How's your Dad?" Franklin asked.

"I don't know. They are still fucking working on him," Anthony answered in a frustrated tone.

Jacob took Anthony's arm and said, "Let's go get some coffee and talk."

"But… my pop?" Anthony replied.

"They'll come and get us when they have news. We need to talk," Jacob said.

The three men walked to the cafeteria and took a table in an isolated corner of the room. One of Jacob's men placed three cups of coffee and a flask on the table, and took a post to ensure no one bothered them. Jacob picked up the flask and pointed it to Anthony's cup. Anthony nodded and Jacob poured the whiskey in all three cups.

Anthony picked up the cup and said, "To my pop." The three men clinked their cups and drank.

"I needed that. Thanks. Now tell me about the motherfucker who shot my father," Anthony said.

"Dead. We have his partner at my place," Jacob said.

"I want to see that fucking bastard and cut his eyes out," Anthony growled.

"We'll keep him on ice until you're ready," Franklin said.

Anthony held his cup out and Jacob poured three more shots from the flask. Anthony drank the contents of the cup and smashed it on the floor.

"That fucking son of a bitch Nitty! I'll kill that cock sucker one day," Anthony screamed.

Several people nearby looked at them and one woman shook her head in admonishment. "Sorry," Franklin said. The woman cocked her head, gave him her best disciplinarian look, and turned back to what she was doing.

"We're with you, Tony. You know that," Jacob said.

Looking past Jacob and seeing his father's doctor walking towards the table, Anthony jumped to his feet and asked in a pleading voice, "How's Pop?"

"It's looking good. The bullet went through his side and out the fleshy part of his back. He'll be okay, but I want him to stay here for a couple of days just to be sure," the doctor explained.

Anthony fell back in his chair and murmured a short prayer of thanks.

"Doc, you're a fucking ace. Can I see him?"

"Sure. He's awake," The doctor replied.

"Tony, go see your pop. Call us when you want to meet our friend," Jacob said.

"I'll call," Anthony said as he left with the doctor.

"You have a pen on you?" Franklin asked Jacob.

"What the fuck do you need a pen for?" Jacob asked as he reached in his suit pocket and handed Franklin a pen.

"Just need to write a note," Franklin said, as he took a napkin and wrote a message on it. He rose and walked over to the woman who had admonished them for Anthony's language. He handed it to her and walked away.

As Franklin and Jacob walked out of the cafeteria, Jacob asked, "What the fuck did you write?"

"I just told her I was sorry and I would like to make it up to her. I left her my phone number," Franklin said.

When Jacob and Franklin returned to the house, Rose's daughters and some close friends were cooking dinner. People would be bringing over meals and cakes for a few more days, as was the custom.

Molly was in the living room with Rose when Jacob entered the room. She jumped up and ran to him, hugging him tightly.

"Thank God!" she exclaimed.

Jacob asked her to sit down on the sofa, and then he sat between her and Rose. He put his arms around both and said, "It's over. We're all safe now. I sent word to have the kids brought home by tomorrow."

Molly took his hand and squeezed it. Rose asked, "Is Don Amato…?" and trailed off, not wanting to say it.

"No, he's fine. He'll be out of the hospital in a couple of days," Jacob answered.

"He saved our lives," Rose said.

"He did. He's a very brave man, Rose. He saved us all," Jacob said.

Jacob stood up and said, "Rose, Frank will stay with you. I need to talk to Molly about arrangements for when the kids come home." He took Molly's hand and they left the room. Jacob guided Molly into their bedroom and closed the door.

Anthony Amato called three hours later as Jacob was getting ready to sit down for dinner. Jacob excused himself and Franklin, and they drove to the Wishart Street house. Jacob glanced up at the plaque he had placed on the corner of the house and felt a wave of pride come over him for his darling Mercy.

Jacob and Franklin took the alley and walked past four yards to the 125 Wishart home. They entered the basement where Mike, Grady and Anthony Amato were waiting. Anthony was standing in front of the getaway man, who was sobbing profusely. As Jacob and Franklin turned to greet Anthony, they saw that the man's left eye socket was bleeding.

"I told you I'd cut his fucking eyes out," Anthony said.

"I need to ask him a question, Tony. Is that okay?"

"Yeah, sure. I didn't cut his tongue out…" Anthony said as he turned towards the man and continued. "Yet." The man turned his head away and whimpered.

"Why did you continue to come after us when your bosses told you not too?" Jacob asked.

Anthony put the knife to the man's good eye. "I don't know nuffin' about that. They just paid us and sent us here. We didn't have a choice," the man said, pleading.

"That's what I thought. That fucking cunt Nitti never called these guys off," Jacob said, pointing at the man.

"Well, that's too bad for you," Anthony said, leaning close to the man's face. "Your buddy shot the Don of the Philly operation. You shot my father, you fucking prick!" Anthony placed the knife on the man's throat and cut left to right, slicing through the windpipe and the carotid artery. Blood spurted as the man shuddered. His eyes bulged and his head fell forward. He was dead.

Anthony undid the man's belt and pulled his pants down. "What the fuck are you doing, Tony?" Jacob asked, alarmed.

"I'm leaving a message." Anthony took the man's cock in his hand and cut it off. He then placed it in the man's mouth and closed it.

"I don't want any more cock suckers from Chicago coming to Philly."

23

Three days later, Jacob and Molly's children were home. Don Amato was out of the hospital and things were starting to return to normal. Molly arranged a dinner for the entire family, including Franklin, Mike, Brian and Grady. Jimmy had come home from college to be with the family.

Rose insisted on cooking. She made Jacob's favorite meal: meatloaf with tomato sauce topping, macaroni and cheese, and an assortment of vegetables. She had even sent Grady to buy fresh ice cream from the Greenwood Dairy in Langhorne.

"I have an announcement to make," Jacob said. Everyone stopped talking and waited for Jacob to continue. "Rose has agreed to run Mercy Row. We start finding families to live in the homes next week."

Mercy ran up to Rose, hugged her, and said, "I am so happy, Grandma Rose! I want to help after school, Dad. Can I? Can I?"

"Sure; it's your foundation, Mercy. I am sure Rose could use the help. I also hired a fellow I met, when Mercy was in the hospital, to help as a handyman. His name is Nate Washington," Jacob said.

"Jimmy, how's school going?" Rose asked.

"Good. I really like it," Jimmy answered.

"What're you taking up?" Grady asked.

"Room, he's taking up room," Franklin said, laughing.

"Funny, Uncle Frank. I'm studying law," Jimmy said.

"Now that's something we can use," Mike said. Jacob and Frank looked at him and Mike continued. "You know for the construction business."

As the banter continued, Jacob felt a sense of contentment for the first time in a long while. His children were growing up and he was proud of how they were turning out. They did well in school and he was sure they would grow up to be successful in a legitimate business. The family was safe. Molly was close to having their fourth child and she was happy. He had good friends like Franklin, more a bother than and friend, and Mike and Grady were loyal to the bone. And with Prohibition gone, the economy should start to get better. The construction company had obtained a few lucrative government contracts, and the Chicago mob had stepped back.

Amato was healing, and their relationship was even stronger than before. The future was looking bright. Peace was here to stay.

"Hey Dad," Jimmy said. "Have you been reading about what's happening in Germany with this Hitler guy?"

Author's Biography

Harry Hallman

Hallman was born in 1944 and raised in the Kensington section of North Philadelphia. His father was Harry Hallman, Sr., a champion billiards player who also owned a poolroom called Circle Billiards, located at Allegany Avenue and Lee Street. The younger Hallman spent many hours after school at his father's pool hall. These youthful experiences laid the groundwork for his novel *Mercy Row*, including the colorful language in the text.

He served four years in the U.S. Air Force, including two tours in South Vietnam as a photographer. He is married to Duoc Hallman, whom he met in Vietnam, and has two children, Bill and Nancy, and one grandchild, Ava.

Hallman is a serial entrepreneur who has created several marketing services companies and continues to work as a marketing consultant.

"My favorite possession, from my childhood, is a baby book my sister gave my mother (Florence) when I was born. There is a passage in this book, written by my mother in 1991 when I was 47, that seems to sum up what I have endeavored to be all my life. It reads, 'Bud [my childhood name] grew up to be a great boy and man. Gruff, but a heart as big as could be.'

Look for the continuation of the Mercy Row story by mid 2013.

Keep informed at www.mercyrow.com or on Facebook at www.facebook.com/mercyrownovel.

Made in the USA
Middletown, DE
10 November 2021